PRAISE FOR
The Passion of Darius

I loved the mixture of historical romance and BDSM. I loved the conflict and inner turmoil I found in **The Passion of Darius**. I loved so much about this book. It reached in and grabbed hold of my heart until I was laughing and crying for both of them.

THE BOOKISH SNOB ~

I could read about Darius and Marianne forever. And as it so happens, Raine's next installment of **The Blackstone Affair**, ***Rare and Precious Things*** , we get more glimpses into the lives of Darius and Marianne through journals discovered in Ethan and Brynne's new home. **The Passion of Darius** is truly a beautiful love story. Darius' love for Marianne is the kind of love every little girl dreams of finding when they grow up.

W. LE GRAND ~

This historical romance from Raine Miller is wonderful. A secret love that has been hidden for years grows more and more intense and all consuming, until an opportunity presents itself for total domination and submission. A love story truly rare and precious.

ANGELA C. ~

I'll just say that it has been a long while since I've actually shed some tears while reading a romance...This story is a keeper for me.

FARAH'S REVIEWS ~

Love, love, love this historical novella by Raine Miller. Having had read *The Blackstone Affair* first, I knew that Ms. Miller's historical romance books had tie-ins to *The Blackstone Affair* and would play a role in future books of that series. I adored Darius *fanning myself* Dominant yet loving, and sensitive and charming to boot. As always with any Raine Miller book, I was not left disappointed.

BECCA THE BIBLIOPHILE ~

Erotic, unrelenting, passionate, and unforgettable. Those are but a few words to describe this novella by Raine Miller. Let's face it, it's been years since I have read historical romances. I moved away from the genre because I wanted a taste of modern life. I will have to reconsider this decision after reading Raine Miller's *The Passion of Darius*. There was nothing about this novella that is not just as relevant today. I would

strongly advise readers to make this part of your reading as you pick up the latest in **The Blackstone Affair ~ *Rare and Precious Things***. I will be on the lookout for more historical romances of this caliber in the future. I am amazed at what I have been missing!

G. HERRERA ~

PRAISE FOR
The Blackstone Affair

Ethan Blackstone is the most swoon-worthy male character I've ever encountered.
COLLEEN HOOVER, New York Times *Bestselling Author ~*

The title of this book is so aptly named as her characters are stripped **Naked** down to their bare feelings and what they do to one another.
FLIRTY & DIRTY BOOK BLOG ~

Erotica with heart has never been so lovely. Although **The Blackstone Affair** is now over, there were some great teases of future writing to come. OH! And also, Millers' book, **The Passion of Darius** has a tie in! **Rare and Precious Things** was a masterful ending to a phenomenal series.
KT BOOK REVIEWS ~

Fast paced, page turner with smart-mouth characters. Leaves you with just enough steam coming out of your panties to keep you hanging on long enough for, **All In**.
EROTIC SMUT REVIEWS ~

Eyes Wide Open is a jaw-dropping, heart-palpitating, pulse-racing thrill ride of emotion, romance, lust, and ultimately, the most unconditional and unforgettable of loves.

KATIE ASHLEY, New York Times *Bestselling Author* ~

Bravo Raine Miller, I slowly savored every word of this gorgeous story, the flow of *Rare and Precious Things* was flawless, and when it was over, I was crying happy tears. I am so emotionally invested in these characters, not only Ethan and Brynne, but all of them. I have thoroughly enjoyed it every step of the way! I would also recommend Ms. Miller's historical books *The Passion of Darius* and *The Undoing of a Libertine*, as there are connections throughout this series that make it so much fun!

J. GERSCHICK ~

I would have to commend Ms. Miller and her magnificent mind. I finished *Rare and Precious Thing*s with tear-stained cheeks ~ one of the best epilogues I have ever read. I was choking back more tears and couldn't stop thinking about it. Raine Miller is at her best in this book. She proves simplicity and two great characters make for the best romances. I couldn't have enjoyed it more. This book perfectly sums up Ethan and Brynne's relationship— Rare and Precious...

"Brynne was my life. The last piece of my puzzle that had finally completed me." -**Ethan Blackstone**

THE BOOK AVENUE ~

Other titles by Raine Miller

The UNDOING of a LIBERTINE

The Blackstone Affair

NAKED

ALL IN

EYES WIDE OPEN

CHERRY GIRL

RARE and PRECIOUS THINGS

THE

Passion

OF

Darius

RAINE MILLER

THE *Passion* OF *Darius*

ISBN: 1496030001
ISBN-13: 978-1496030009

DEDICATION

For my beautiful family

"I have crossed oceans of time to find you."

~Dracula to Mina

CONTENTS

ACKNOWLEDGMENTS

My path to becoming a writer began with this little book. The voices spoke to me until they had to come out onto the page. I don't quite know exactly when that magical transformation occurred but I do know that it happened with this story. And for that I will always hold dear my gratefulness for these two special lovers finding their way into my life. Darius is special for another reason—and he knows why. His name is the *first* word of my *first* story ever to see the light of day. *Firsts* are important…

If you are not already aware, there is a connection between **The Passion of Darius** and my **Blackstone Affair** series. The books are linked through people and place over nearly two hundred years. Especially book four in that series, **Rare and Precious Things**. *winks* You'll just have to read to find out how.

My eternal thanks to all of the lovely fans who write to me and inspire me to create characters that they can enjoy, sharing right along with them on their journeys of loving and hurting, suffering and growing, redeeming and forgiveness. What could be better, right? *waves and blows kisses*

xxoo *Raine*

CHAPTER 1

The Declaration

Somerset Coast, 1837

Darius chose his seat strategically every Sunday. Close enough to catch her scent just from sitting behind her in church. He waited for it, knowing what would come, for he was familiar with her choice of perfume. The soft essence of violets floated to him, its delicate sweetness stirring and calming both at once. Savoring the instant when he could draw even the tiniest part of her into himself, Darius indulged in the simple pleasure of breathing her.

Her neck was his favorite. He loved to look at the place where her coffee-colored hair swept up with just a few strands escaping. Indulging in wild dreams about her, he imagined how she'd look with all those glorious waves spilling down over her pale, naked flesh. Of how he would brush it aside and put his lips to that spot he so desired to know. He thought of the triumph of possessing her totally. Of her soft, pliant body beneath his hard, commanding one, accepting him inside when he took her.

Wanting her so badly was nothing new. He'd known the feeling for a long time. Marianne was perfection in Darius's opinion.

Marianne might be perfect, but her father was an idiot. Mr. George was a weak man. He had turned to drink after the death of his wife, bringing them to the brink of ruin with his drinking and gambling. At the pace he was going, Darius figured her father's descent would sit well with his own plans regardless. Being a patient man, Darius didn't think he would have to wait much longer. Her father would see to that for him.

THE hair on the back of her neck tingled and she knew. His eyes were on her. Again. Marianne looked around as soon as the service ended. Yes, indeed. He stood there staring—his dark eyes calling her to meet his gaze.

Her father nodded politely at him. "Mr. Rourke, good day."

"Mr. George. Miss Marianne, you look well today." Mr. Rourke greeted both of them warmly, but his eyes rested only on her.

"Yes, sir, my Marianne is very fine. She takes after her mother, God rest her soul." He crossed himself. "I daresay there's not any more beautiful to be found in all of Somerset," he boasted.

Marianne wanted to crawl under a pew in mortification. Why did Papa say such things? His thinly disguised attempt to throw her into the path of a wealthy gentleman such as Darius Rourke was grossly inappropriate. She felt her neck flush with heat.

"Papa, please!" She pulled at her father's arm to lead him away. Offering a sympathetic look to Mr. Rourke, she mouthed a silent, "I am sorry," for her father's boorishness before turning to leave.

"What? Can a father not want the best for his child? He admires you! It would serve you well to encourage him, lass!" He practically shouted his opinions at Marianne as she led him out to the churchyard. Mr. Rourke would have to be deaf not to have heard.

"Shhh, Papa!" She vowed silently to skip church next Sunday for she didn't know how she could face Mr. Rourke after this horrifying display.

Something compelled her to turn around. And Marianne knew exactly what would be waiting when she did.

Still standing in the same spot, tracking her, Mr. Rourke smiled, his perception all-knowing, as if he'd been assured she'd turn back to him.

Oh, dear God! I must be in hell.

At least a decade older than her, Mr. Rourke was a quiet man, possessing an air of mystery that hinted at the level of intensity to his character, but remained properly veiled under the gentlemanly comportment of his station. He conveyed a subtle influence in most of his dealings with others, not entirely discernible in anything he said or did, but recognizable nonetheless. Marianne thought him handsome. With his noble features, he attracted the notice of many women. Tall and broad shouldered, he filled out his fine European suits brilliantly. His skin held a darker cast than was typical for an Englishman, a golden hue that complemented the dark hair and eyes perfectly. He was simply beautiful.

But male beauty aside, Darius Rourke wasn't for her. No man was for her.

Marianne couldn't fathom why he would even show an interest. Her upbringing had been respectable enough, a gentleman's daughter, but their situation had declined perilously in recent years. Her dowry had long since gone by way of drink and cards. Papa had seen to that. Marianne shuddered, thinking about the debts Papa incurred on his forays into town.

Still, whenever their paths crossed, Mr. Rourke made a

point to pay her specific courtesy and deference. He was never anything less than a gentleman in his behavior towards her, but Marianne detected an undercurrent. There was something about his attentions that unsettled her. Thoroughly. Like he could peer right inside her and know her every thought. When he cast those flashing dark eyes of his in her direction she felt exposed and vulnerable, on the verge of being devoured. By him.

He might even be more aware of her "need" than she thought, from the way his gaze could penetrate. After an encounter with him she always came away feeling a little shaken, breathless, and confounded.

IT took the passing of another month before Marianne's father ruined them completely. This pleased Darius for it worked into his plans rather seamlessly.

Darius summoned father and daughter to his home under the guise of a summer picnic. With lunch *al fresco*, and then strawberry picking, he figured an opportunity would likely result. There would be others attending as well, of course, friends and neighbors, Mr. Jeremy Greymont, the Rothvales, the Bleddingtons, and the Carstones.

Darius felt himself harden just from the thought of spending so many hours with her so close. It was becoming a challenge for him to control the urges. Yes, Miss Marianne George would be here at his home this day, and he knew the time for waiting was over. She was coming for a picnic, true, but he had other plans in mind for his Marianne.

Yes, mine.

Darius could not help the sway of his heart. He wanted Marianne and only her, for he found her to be perfect, meant for him in a way that prevented him from considering any other but her. He dreamed about her constantly. Dreamed of making her his, of claiming her, making love to her, envisioning his body all over her body, of being inside her. His dreams of Marianne were always erotic and very vivid. These and similar thoughts of Marianne George obsessed him.

He'd only come back to Somerset a mere six months ago, after being away for years. Darius had thought he might have put his infatuation for Marianne George aside during the long absence, but that'd proved false the second he'd laid eyes on her again.

Waiting for her had been a challenge while she grew up. And through the years he'd ever admired her, she was forever in his head, tempting him mercilessly. Now she had grown up a most beautiful woman, unattached to any man and ready to be plucked. He thought her silky, dark hair, blue eyes, and lush figure magnificent, but there were other reasons for the attraction.

She did not throw herself at him, as many other young ladies tried to do. Marianne George was a complex young woman, and Darius was sure he understood the reason. There was more to her than youthful beauty, much more.

She had fire in her waiting to be stoked. This he could tell. He also suspected that submitting to him, to his dominance, would appeal to her. He'd noticed that he could make her look at him when he stared at her, and that she definitely waited for his gaze. The looks she returned mesmerized him. Her eyes smoldered, like burning embers waiting for a rush of air to fan them into flame.

Darius was certain. The dominance would be lovingly bestowed of course. If Marianne craved it, then he needed to be the one to give it to her. He would offer to her that which she desired.

MARIANNE'S cheeks burned hot. She could only imagine the deep color of her blush. Sitting right next to her, she could sense Mr. Rourke's eyes staring because her neck tingled. Nothing new there. This game they'd been playing had gone on for weeks and needed to cease. Today.

She braved a glance. His dark eyes glittered at her. He smiled as if he'd expected her to look. She grasped at anything to say and came up with very little except, "The day is lovely. You picked a good one for your party, Mr. Rourke."

"Yes…so lovely," he answered, his eyes roaming over her.

She got the impression he wasn't referring to the weather and felt supremely stupid. She would do better just to keep her mouth closed before more half-witted nonsense left it.

"I'm so happy you're here, Miss Marianne. I hope today is just the first of many visits."

She shook her head. "Oh, I don't—"

"I say it's time for the berry picking! They're sweetest when the sun is high," Miss Byrony Everley announced her opinion to the group.

Marianne thought her dear friend's interruption especially timely.

"Byrony! It's Mr. Rourke's party and for him to say," her mother admonished.

"No worries, Lady Rothvale," he said, rising from the grass. "I am not in the least offended, and I venture that Miss Byrony's suggestion is a good one." His voice turned rich and his words slower. "I'd hate for the full sweetness of the strawberries to be missed." And then he looked right at Marianne's mouth.

Oh, dear God! Marianne swallowed hard, thinking she was in very deep trouble.

"'Twould be a tragedy to pass up the sweet." He held his hand down to her. "Shall we?"

She couldn't refuse him. Not in front of everyone. Mr. Rourke was her host, and it would be rude not to defer to his desire to accompany her. Marianne put her hand out and felt it clasped in a warm grip. Maybe more than warm. His skin was hot—melting hot. He pulled her effortlessly up to standing, right at his chin.

Damn her if she didn't look up at his rich, brown eyes again. What in the world was wrong with her? She didn't want his attentions! Darius Rourke rattled her soundly. He had a way of making her forget why she couldn't receive him. She supposed the time was nearing that she'd have to tell him so. But for right now she calmly accepted the basket he handed over to her and watched as he got one for himself, and before she knew it, was being led with the others, down the path to the glade with her arm wrapped through his.

Idiot!

DARIUS felt he could be in heaven, or possibly as close as he would ever get. For the moment, he had Marianne all to himself. Slowly, he'd steered her away from the others to where he thought the quietness might relax her a little. Darius didn't fool himself. He knew she was wary of him and realized that if his plan were to work he'd have to earn her trust.

He found Marianne mesmerizing and could just watch her unendingly. He admired how graceful her hands were; watching as her fingers gently pushed aside green leaves to search for the heart-shaped fruit. She parted her lips just a bit whenever she found a cache of berries hidden beneath the greenery. The pleasure of observing as she ate a few of the berries had been the definite high point. Marianne had a beautiful mouth.

"Oh! A blackberry vine has pushed in over here," she said.

Darius came right to where she peered into the tangle, standing just behind her shoulder. "They grow as wild as weeds, sprouting up in new spots each year, so I'm not surprised." A few errant curls had come loose, and there was a bit of leaf right above her ear.

Delectable.

He wanted his lips right above her ear so he could flick out his tongue and get a taste of her. What would she taste like? He had to force himself to respond coherently. "But it's a tad early for blackberries yet. By the end of July they'll be bursting with sweet juice. You'll come back then," he told her.

Her spine stiffened, and she faced him. Little creases marred her brow. "Mr. Rourke, you mustn't presume that I—"

"—only an invitation to pick berries, Miss Marianne, and only if you wish it," he said smoothly. He disarmed her with his response. He could see it happen and knew the second she regretted her comment, as clearly as if he could see inside her head.

"Of course it is." Her blue eyes swept down. "Please forget I said anything."

Impossible to forget anything about you.

He reached out his hand, helpless to restrain himself. Darius was going to touch her. She saw what he meant to do, though, and reacted by backing right up and away from him. He followed her anyway, deftly plucking the small, dry leaf from her hair.

He held it up to show her. "You had this trapped in your hair."

"Ahhh," she breathed out, looking relieved. "Th—thank you, Mr. Rourke. We should probably go back now," she said softly, her eyes fluttering down once again.

The urge to take her further into the berry thicket and kiss her senseless flashed as a possibility, but sanity overruled it.

"As you wish." He offered his arm. They had not taken even a step before the rending of fabric sounded below them.

"Oh blast! The brambles have caught me!" She turned, reaching for the thorny vine imbedded in her skirt.

"Careful! You don't want to get—"

"Ouch!" she cried.

"—pricked."

The basket dropped to the ground in a rush as she gripped her injured hand, palm-up.

"Here, let me." He took her hand for inspection. A large thorn was indeed buried in the pad of her index finger, the black strip a garish invader on such lovely skin. "I'll get it for you. Hold still and squeeze your finger on the sides as I remove it." She followed his directions perfectly and hardly winced when he pulled the thorn away. A bead of dark blood chased the thorn, welling up red on the pad of her finger.

Darius couldn't help what he did next. His mind and body were operating independently of the other, and he just reacted without conscious thought of how he would be perceived. Before he knew it, he had her hand drawn to his lips and was sucking the blood away. Earthy spice met his tongue and the merest moan escaped him. Her horrified gasp followed his moan. She jerked her finger away.

"Mr. Rourke!" she scolded, frowning at him before dropping down to retrieve the strawberry basket.

He couldn't hold in the grin and bent down to help her with the berries. "Sorry. I assure you I am no vampire."

She looked up at him sharply. "You don't look very sorry. About being a demon, I'm sure I couldn't comment."

She was flustered and irritated with him and so utterly adorable it required everything he had to refrain from pulling her against him and taking her mouth. In her present state he might just get a smack if he did though.

"Just trying to close the wound, and I am indeed sorry for your injury," he told her. "Now, if you'll stand still, I'll get this vine detached from your skirt."

Her soft breathing came faster as he worked on the blackberry thorns. She obeyed and stood still for him, but her lush body trembled mightily in response underneath all those layers. God, it would be good between them—all the sex. He told himself to focus on the goal. It was time to tell her.

"At the conclusion of the party today, I've asked your father to stay. I have some business to discuss with him, and I'd like for you to be present as well, Miss Marianne."

She nodded once in agreement. "We must go back now, Mr. Rourke." He could tell she had been pushed as far as she would go…for now.

"Of course we must." He smiled down at her.

She didn't speak again for the rest of the party. That was fine. Darius could enjoy her simply by having her near…for now.

"THOUGH your amount of debt is ruinous, Mr. George, I have a solution. It will be much preferable to debtors' prison, I think."

"What can I do for you, Mr. Rourke?" Mr. George slurred, probably half-sprung from all the wine he'd taken during the day.

"Give your consent to Marianne's marriage to me." He saw the shock in her expression at his proposal. Her eyes rolled up, her lips parted, and her breath grew shallow. *Perfect.* "Your debts will be paid, an allowance provided you, and Marianne will be settled respectably, protected and cared for as my wife."

"Of course, Mr. Rourke, you may have *my* consent. She'll marry you," Mr. George agreed eagerly.

"No! Papa, you cannot make me!" Marianne faced Darius, her lovely blue eyes sparking at him. "Sir, I have no wish to marry. A decision I have made long ago. I am not suited for marriage. Your offer is flattering, but I will not be able to accept you."

The thrill is already beginning, and you are so wrong. You are perfectly suited.

Right now, her regal stance, glinting eyes, and flushed cheeks all combined into one glorious vision. Her throat rising and falling with anxious breathing, causing strands of silky hair to flutter about her head, transfixed him. He wanted to press his lips to her neck and draw her to him. She might say she didn't want it, but he believed she did. She just needed some convincing, was all. He could do that. The art of persuasion was a skill he possessed in abundance. Darius instinctively knew the way to get to her was through her father.

He changed his voice, directing it only to her. "Miss Marianne, would it not be easing to put your troubles aside? Let your cares and worries be placed into the hands of another? Into *my* willing hands? I would never wish for you to feel you had been coerced or forced in any way to do something that you could not reconcile yourself to. My offer is an honorable one. It is time for me to marry, and I greatly admire you."

He paused at seeing her swallow hard, her neck pulsing in the hollow below her jaw. "I believe you are aware of that, and I also believe you would be the perfect partner for me. I approve of the manner in which you conduct yourself and your...disposition. There is no avarice in you."

He turned to look disparagingly at Mr. George. "Your father's debt is grave though. In a matter of days you will be out of your home, forced into debtors' prison. But such a horrifying fate doesn't have to be yours. I hate to think of you being subjected to such harsh conditions. And yes, Marianne, you would have to go, to look after your father. Is that what you would choose? Prison? Over marriage to me?"

He asked his questions gently, knowing exactly how to appeal to her need for direction and guidance at this moment of self-possession. "I think you want to marry me, don't you, Marianne?"

"Sir, why would you do this?" Marianne shook her head unbelievingly.

Because I must have you.

"You suit me, Marianne. You are beautiful and elegant, and know your duty. You always do the right thing, because you are good, and you never want to disappoint."

She looked at him. So silent, solemn, and utterly magnificent.

He whispered the last very softly. "Don't disappoint me, Marianne."

CHAPTER 2

The Acceptance

W hen she heard him say, "Don't disappoint me," Marianne realized he knew. Somehow Mr. Rourke was aware of her desires. He'd watched her for so long, he'd puzzled her out. He knew what words to say and how to phrase them. And Mr. Rourke seemed to be the kind of man prepared to persist until he got his way. She realized this as well. He sought to compel her and tell her what to do. He wanted dominion over her. But Mr. Rourke was wrong about one part. Not always did she do the right thing. Sometimes she did wrong. Very wrong.

Marianne felt the walls closing in. The air in the room seemed to grow heavy as he stared into her eyes. She couldn't do this. It wasn't right for her to want—

"Mr. Rourke, I cannot accept your offer. It is—it's not possible for me to be your—"

She stopped and shook her head at him, and then even had to turn away. She had almost said it out loud for God's sake! It simply wasn't possible for her to be a wife. She wasn't fit for the role. Matrimony would not be her destiny, and it'd be best if she made that fact clear to him right now. He wouldn't want her anyway if he knew what she'd done. Darius Rourke was a man of wealth and property and needed heirs to pass it along. He must have a wife sensible in mind and capable of rearing his children, and that person certainly wouldn't be her. She must not even consider such a notion.

If she allowed him to bore into her eyes a second longer, she'd lose her resolve. She had to get out of here. Her instincts screamed at her to get away from him and his commanding presence before he spoke another word! He was too good at coercion. Their little dance around the berry patch earlier had proved just how good he was. And the problem was that she liked when he directed her. Far too much.

"Papa, we are leaving." She took her father by the arm and led him out. At the door, she paused, feeling a cold shiver rattle up the back of her neck.

"You disappoint me, Marianne." His voice had a hard edge now. That Darius Rourke did not like being told "no" was of little surprise.

Marianne froze, closing her eyes, praying for strength. Without turning back, she whispered, "I am sorry, Mr. Rourke. I just cannot—" Stumbling on through the doorway; she fled his house, pulling her father along with her.

AS soon as his guests departed, Darius took paper from his desk and began to write. He was calm but resolute when he called for his steward and gave instructions for delivery of the missive.

She'd surprised him with her refusal. This time. He wasn't really all that concerned though. There were means at his disposal to be more persuasive. This was something he could do. If it meant winning her, he could do just about anything. Yes, Marianne George may have just turned him down, be he'd felt, no, *seen,* a crack in that armor she covered herself in. Darius would be more successful next time, getting under her skin, forcing her to acknowledge him, to accept him. He would have her acquiescence. No other alternative was tolerable.

MARIANNE looked around the room. The destruction of her life was clearly visible and she wanted to weep. But that was just self-pitying indulgence, wasn't it? And she could truly say that the wreck of her family was all her fault anyway.

Papa was sprawled out on the chaise, foxed to the gills. The eviction notice he'd read, crumpled on the floor. A bailiff had served it into her hands this very day.

Three days was all the time they had. In three days he'd return with officers of the court to see they were taken to the Marshalsea in London. She picked it up and read it again. Unpaid debts were a crime under the law. Papa was a…criminal. There was only one creditor listed and that seemed odd, and the name was not one she even recognized.

Grasping at any solution, she thought about a way out. Maybe Lord Rothvale might be inclined to help. He was influential and very kind. She'd known him all her life, and his daughter, Byrony, was one of her best friends. She threw up her hands in frustration. What was she thinking? She could never impose upon friends in such a way.

Marianne left the house. She had to get outside and go look at the ocean. Her legs felt weak as she made her way, but the closer she came to the majestic expanse of brine, the stronger her resolve grew. Once the glassy blue of the water was in her sights, she breathed out a sigh. The sea soothed her and always had. It comforted in a way for which there was no substitute. It had always been so for her. She made her way to the rocky shore, seeking that which would ease her, until she was leaning against a large rock at the mouth of the jetty. She allowed herself to remember.

Shame was the worst of it. She wasn't worried about what they'd have to endure in the Marshalsea. It was the shame that killed her. That and the cruel fact of knowing even if they went to prison, it still wouldn't change anything. Jonathan wasn't coming back to her. Papa wouldn't be restored to his former respectable self. Mamma was gone forever. The ravagement of her life was complete, and nothing was going to put it back to rights. She mourned the loss and realized suddenly the ache and despair of knowing she'd never be free of her guilt.

She wouldn't even have this—the comfort of the sea. That would be the hardest part to give up. She let the tears come and tried to memorize every sense in moment. The smell of salt and seaweed, the whip of the breeze chilling the tears on her cheeks, the sounds of the churning water and flapping of her dress, the variant colors of blue.

Can you hear me, Jonathan? We're going to be leaving…soon, and I won't be able to come here anymore. I'm so sorr—

"It doesn't have to be like this, Marianne."

Marianne snapped her head around and then quickly down, brushing at her tears with a knuckle. "Mr. Rourke!

21

You startled me, sir." She turned away so he couldn't see her face. Why had he come out here? Had he seen her and followed?

"I apologize for startling you, but not for my words."

Marianne didn't answer or acknowledge his apology. She just kept staring out at the sea. The wind and the waves buffeted the rocks below, as they had done for eons. *Jonathan?*

"I saw that the bailiff paid you a visit and I know why he was there."

Of course he knew why. The whole village probably knew already. Any words of acknowledgement still refused to come from her mouth. What could she possibly say anyway? Frozen in place, she continued to do what she'd been doing before he'd come out here to confront her. She faced into the wind and churning surf and stayed silent.

"My God, Marianne. Prison! You'll have to live in a filthy prison! A dirty, defiled, infested prison, miles away from your home and that which you've known your whole life!"

I know.

She nodded imperceptibly, still unable to look at him. "Did you follow me out here just to throw that in my face?" She spoke toward the sea and thought it very cruel of him to voice it even though she'd been the one to reject him and he was probably still angry.

"No. I did not," he said more gently.

"Then why are you here, Mr. Rourke?"

"To remind you that it is in your power to stop this madness, Marianne. You can stop it. You know what you *could* do. The question is—will you do it? Will you?" His voice burned through the ocean breeze.

Oh, dear God! Could she have heard him correctly? He still wanted her? Even after she'd refused him? A proud man like him, willing to offer again, even in her low situation? Unbelievable. Still she remained frozen, afraid to look.

"Look at me, sweet Marianne. Show your beautiful face to me."

She started to breathe heavily. A warm flush penetrated and began to tingle through her. He had moved closer and was now standing right behind her. So close she could smell the spice of his cologne.

"Do it. Turn around and look up at me. You want to, Marianne. I know you do," he whispered, near enough that his breath kissed her neck.

He was right. She did want to. Turning to face him, a warm heat flooded between her legs. She saw him inhale as if to scent her. A curl of a smile lifted on his mouth and his eyes burned.

"You've been crying." He fished out his handkerchief and pressed it gently to each cheek. "I don't like you crying. And I think I know why you were." He leaned down closer. "Let me take care of you. Your father, too. You'll want for nothing." He tilted his head, honing in on her. "Marry me."

Telling her what to do didn't seem to be a problem for him. He smiled and slowly nodded, willing her to accept him. He was boldly telling her to agree, but did it in such a way that she *wanted* to agree. Lord, he was handsome! A lock of glossy black hair slipped down over his forehead, and she had the urge to reach out and smooth it back. What would his hair feel like?

Mr. Rourke had her ensnared without a doubt, and he was very skilled at seduction. Marianne accepted that resisting him was a futile enterprise on her part. Her desire was far too formidable of a beast to conquer. It felt enormously relieving to yield to him. His lilting voice, like cool silk brushing over warm skin, told her exactly what she wanted to do.

And if she was honest with herself, she could admit to the pure comfort to be had in embracing his dominance. Soothing. Relieving. Oh, yes. Feelings she had never allowed herself to indulge in. He would be *good* for her in that way. And more importantly, a marriage with Darius Rourke would enable her to save Papa. This marriage would provide a way, albeit insufficient, to partially atone for what she'd done.

Resolving to accept his offer before she might change her mind, she straightened her posture. A shiver and a breathy sigh escaped at the thought of belonging to him. The way he looked at her. Imagining what he'd do with her! She was certainly a mouse caught in the paws of an indomitable, pouncing cat. And when the time came for the cat to devour the mouse, Marianne prayed she'd not regret her choice.

"Mr. Rourke, I—I do agree. I'll marry you."

"Yes?" His eyes lit up with glittering sparks at her answer, spurring her to speak resolutely.

"I will."

Marianne would not forget the look upon his face when she gave him her agreement. Darius Rourke looked very…pleased, which, again, mystified her as to why he found her so attractive. She prayed he wouldn't regret this decision any more than she might.

THAT'S my good girl. You want it. I was right about you.

He took her hand and brought it forward. His lips kissed the cool skin of her hand as his thumb caressed over her elegant fingers. The essence of her flesh so close threatened to overpower his senses. Darius let the desire seize him—the tightening down low as the blood hardened him to iron. God, it felt good. He could stand here staring, breathing in her delicate scent, nibbling her skin, forever and never get tired of it. Just having her close felt like a reward. He kissed her hand a second time, lingering a little longer with his lips, drawing in her natural essence through the softness of her silky skin.

"You have made me *very* happy, Marianne. Let's go tell your father the good news."

Her luminous blue eyes looking up moved him deeply. She was beautiful to him. And now she'd be his. He would be the one—the one to discover her secrets.

Anticipating how he would take her the first time made him lightheaded. Her innocence required a gentle hand of course. And he would gladly give it. Darius would be so very careful with her initiation into the pleasures of the flesh. But still, his need to know her was nearly uncontainable. In his imaginings, he experienced lurid visions of possessing her beautiful body in so many ways, of satisfying his desires finally, after years of wanting her.

MARIANNE sat down that night and began to write. The journal had been given to her by her mother. One of the last gifts she'd ever received from her before she was gone. Mamma had said it was admirable for a lady to put down her thoughts on paper. Marianne pondered upon what she had agreed to this afternoon, and once again, could not see how she would manage to be all that her future husband believed she would be.

7th May, 1837

   ...Today I also gave my agreement to marry a man who says he wants nothing more than to care for me and to allow him to cherish me. He looks into my eyes and touches a part of my soul in a way that terrifies me, yet at the same time draws me in deeper to understand his motivation. I believe he can see into part of my secret. He understands me, because his words cut right to the essence of my problem, leaving me no choice but to give in to his demands.

   So I will go to live at Stonewell Court and make my life with him...but I am very afraid of what awaits me. How will I ever rise to the standard of what is expected of me? I am not worthy, and I fear my carefully guarded heart is in great danger of being shattered beyond the ability for it to continue to beat within my breast. Darius Rourke doesn't yet understand that I do not deserve to be cherished by any man. I am torn, and yet he is persuasively persistent in continuing to assure me all will be well, and to trust in him.

   I find myself unable to deny Darius in his wishes for me, just as I was unable to deny my beloved Jonathan...
MG

CHAPTER 3

The Kiss

Marianne realized Darius felt entitled to demand a little more since she was now his betrothed. Their engagement had been announced, but it would be three weeks yet until they married. As her fiancé, he could call upon her and sit next to her in church. And he took full advantage of those opportunities. He held her hand and kissed it, walked with her, and often sent her letters and gifts.

"I have something for you, Marianne." He presented a slim, leather volume into her hands.

Opening to the title page, she smiled when she saw the inscription he'd written. *To my Marianne, From your Darius.* She hardly knew what to say. Did Darius think of himself as belonging to her? It was a very intimate thought, and

Marianne felt a thrill of pleasure at him believing in it. He really was so lovely to her all the time.

"John Keats. His poetry is beautiful. I will enjoy this very much. Thank you, Dar—Mr. Rourke."

"I think you want to call me *Darius*." He nodded slowly at her. "And now, you want to kiss me, Marianne." Still nodding, he smiled knowingly.

He told you what to do, and now you must do it. Marianne felt another thrill at what he'd just said she must do.

Her breath grew heavy, her heart sped up, but she tilted her mouth toward his. Pushing up on her toes, her soft lips pressed against his firmer ones, and she felt the heat, a shuddering slice of arousal that shot right up between her thighs. A yielding breath escaped before she broke contact of their lips. She kept her lips close to his though. Marianne lifted her eyes to his burning ones.

"Darius," she whispered. Just that short union of lips was shattering, and not nearly enough. He smelled divine, his cologne carrying a hint of exotic spice mixed with fresh linen and…heavenly male. To be so close to him stirred her blood. She let herself be drawn in easily and wondered what else he might ask of her. A shiver brushed over her shoulders and down her spine.

"Say it again."

"Darius…" His name coming off her lips felt lovely.

His eyes flared as he descended for another kiss. This time his mouth moved on hers, warm and soft, but commanding. He nipped at her bottom lip, pulling it into his mouth partway, like he wanted to devour her. She was going to allow him. Unable to resist, she leaned into his kisses, letting him tug her into his mouth, wondering where this would lead.

Darius didn't demand anything more though. At least, not today. He stopped and just smiled, looking pleased when he brought the back of his hand to her face and stroked gently.

"You are something so perfect, Marianne."

No, I am something so definitely not!

WHEN his elegant carriage came to collect her, there was an envelope lying on the leather seat.

Dearest Marianne,

When you go today to be fitted for your wedding clothes, I have arranged for you to select new gowns and assorted garments from the modiste in town. She is French, and will guide you in selecting those items I wish for you to have. Dressing a woman is like framing a beautiful work of art. You, my dear, are the art, and so you must be framed, magnificently. Madame Trulier will have some things ready to take home with you today. Wear them for me, Marianne. I cannot wait to see you dressed as I believe is your due.

Yours,

D. R.

Reading his letter, she became flushed. The thought of Darius picturing her body in want of clothing was very intimate and made her heated. He always did that to her. His words, the looks, the smiles, the barest touch, all served to enflame her until she was unable to think or do anything other than what he asked of her. Darius understood her. Now, when she looked at him, she didn't see a man that was not for her. Rather, she saw a man she wanted to please. She needed to. Compelled to do those things that satisfied him, she was bound to do what he asked of her.

Darius made her feel special in a way she had never experienced before. He cherished her in words and in deeds. Giving in to him felt comforting, and more importantly, safe. He would make sure she did the right things. If she followed his directions she wouldn't be able to make terrible mistakes. Marianne couldn't afford to make another one. Another mistake, like the one with Jonathan, would be the end of her.

Measuring tape in hand, Madame Trulier looked Marianne over carefully. Stripped down to her chemise, her body seemed to be met with approval.

"You are blessed in your figure, my dear. I can see why Mr. Rourke is so enchanted by your charms. We must arrange to show you off to your greatest advantage. Your fiancé was quite specific in what he wants, especially in regards to *dishabille* dress and undergarments. Mr. Rourke said only French silk for your chemises, stockings, and corsets. We shall please him, hmmm? You will be lucky to have such a husband—one who takes an interest."

Marianne chose from those garments suggested by Madame Trulier. There were morning gowns, lounging wrappers, and gorgeous undergarments. Day dresses, evening gowns, riding outfits, and cloaks. Madame insisted on several nightdresses sewn of the sheerest fabrics—beautiful, but capable of concealing little. Marianne felt the blushing heat fill her again when she pictured herself wearing them for Darius.

"He chose this shawl for you. You will take it with you when you go," Madame Trulier announced.

The heavy shawl was a work of art in sea-blue Indian silk, woven in an intricate design, shot through with violet, lavender, and dark purple, iridescent threads. Marianne loved it. The dancing fringe swayed delicately when she caressed her hand over his striking gift. Suddenly swamped with the desire to wear this shawl for Darius, she wanted him to see her wearing it and know she had done it for him, to please him.

I am unable to resist his allure and he well knows it.

The Passion of Darius

7th June, 1837

He has ensnared me. He is as aware of this, as am I. Darius knows how to be with me. He's chosen garments for me to wear. Intimate things that I know he imagines on my body. I love the blue silk shawl best of all. I will always think of the sea when I wear it...and J. He is over-generous and makes me feel so pampered already; and I can freely admit that the feelings his generosity brings about in me, are not easy to rationalize. Darius will have me completely captivated before long. I cannot deny him anything he asks of me now. The time for that has well passed.

MG

CHAPTER 4

The Promise

"Mr. Rourke to see Miss George," Darius told the housemaid.

Too many minutes later, Mr. George stumbled into the room, announcing that Marianne was not at home.

"And where has she gone?"

"Walking along the shore, most likely."

"Alone? She goes alone?" Darius frowned.

Mr. George snorted. "That girl has a mind of her own. I have never been able to break her stubbornness," he said, chuckling. "You're sure to have your hands very full with her, Mr. Rourke. She'll be all yours to worry over soon enough, eh?"

What a stupid man you are, and not much of a father either.

No wonder Marianne is as she is.

Darius abruptly took his leave, heading for the sea path. The thought of her alone, exposed to possible harm, terrified him.

At the rise, he scanned the sandy beach down below. There she was, looking out over the ocean. He'd seen her like this before, the wind rippling her clothes and hair forward. It looked as if the ocean worked in tandem with the wind, calling to her, pulling her in. She wore the shawl. Relief washed over him, and Darius embraced it as wonderfully welcome.

He approached, keeping his eyes trained upon her lovely neck. She must have heard his footsteps because she turned. Her eyes widened in recognition, and then they lit in a look that could only be described as happy to see him. The feelings of relief gave way to ones of sheer joy.

"Darius." She held out her hand in greeting.

He brought it to his lips first. Then he had to touch her. His thumb rubbed back and forth over her knuckles as he inhaled, thinking how her scent calmed his agitation. "I called, but you were not there." He hoped the disapproval in his tone rang clear, though. He needed Marianne to understand.

"Yes. I wanted to walk, and think."

"What occupied your thoughts?"

"You. Marrying you."

That made him smile. "Good thoughts, I hope? Tell me you were thinking good thoughts of me."

"I was, Darius." She blushed and then looked up. "I was thinking good thoughts of you."

He brushed the side of his finger up her cheek. "Marianne, I don't care for you walking out alone here. There are too many dangers, and I would see you kept safe. So, no more solitary walks along the jetty. Agreed?" She regarded him solemnly. "Say, 'I'll not walk alone again, Darius.' Say those words to me, Marianne."

"I'll not walk alone again, Darius."

That's my girl.

He rewarded her with another smile. "You are very dear to me. If you wish to walk, send a note to the house. I will be happy to escort you."

"As you wish." She inclined her head. "Will you walk with me now?"

"Of course." He pulled her arm over his, enveloping her hand in his much larger one. "Your new dress is lovely on you."

He looked her over appreciatively, proud to have her on his arm, and feeling irrationally possessive. He didn't like her out here alone, where anyone could approach her. Kilve had a steady tourist crowd, especially in the summer months. No telling who could be out on the beach. This idea alone, regardless of the natural dangers, made his blood boil. She was his woman. His! And in a matter of days, she'd *truly* belong to him. Visions flashed through his mind. Scenes of her naked, hair down, splayed underneath him, her body wrapped around his cock—

"—Thank you, the clothes are very fine and beautiful." Her sincere words of gratitude dragged him reluctantly out of the erotic reverie he'd dreamed. Shaking his head slightly, he strove to clear his head by focusing on what she was saying. "And, Darius, I love this shawl that you picked for me. It's very special, so unique, and the most gorgeous gift I have ever received. It reminds me of the sea."

"Knowing you are enjoying it thrills me." He stared at her, unable to look away. "In this moment, you look so beautiful, Marianne, with that shawl wrapped around you and the wind making your hair dance. The color matches your eyes. When I saw it, I knew it was meant for you."

"Thank you for the compliment, and for such lovely gifts, Darius."

"Do you wear your new garments next to your skin?"

She breathed in sharply at his question. "I do."

"Why do you wear them?" he whispered, anticipating her answer.

"Because…you told me to."

A shot of pure lust burned through to his groin, and he felt an erection punch out, instantly hard. Marianne didn't realize how her gentle surrender enflamed him. And she gave it so freely, and with such ease, that Darius was utterly entrammeled by her charms. Where he was hard, she was soft. He took, she gave. He commanded, she acquiesced. Darius wondered if she knew he was really like a fly, tangled in her web, stuck fast, going nowhere. Marianne was an addiction, and yet, seemed to have no idea of the potency of her allure.

Stopping her on the path, he leaned down toward her sweet lips. Heat boiled up the instant their mouths connected. This time he would know more of her…

"Kiss me back," he commanded.

He needed to get inside her somehow! So he pushed his tongue along her lips, entreating her to open to him. Slowly, but with firm control, he pressed inside, feeling the returned brush of her soft tongue dueling with his. Tasting. Seeking. Filling. Their tongues mated. The feel of her sent his cock into a desperate state. Having any part of him inside her body was nirvana.

Finally dragging away from her mouth for long enough to form words, he asked, "I can taste strawberries. Did you eat some?"

"I did. At luncheon I had a few." She blushed at him again.

"So sweet you taste. Sweet like a strawberry. I want to feed strawberries to you. I'll put it right into your mouth." He imagined holding a ripe, red strawberry to her lips and her biting into it.

The lovely image gave Darius inspiration of how to get

into her in another way. Using his thumb, he brushed over her lips in a circle before pressing against her teeth. She opened against the pressure, accepting his thumb into her mouth, her tongue wrapping around it, sucking lightly. Darius moved his thumb in and out, slowly, her lips stretching outward when he pulled out, and retreating inward when he pushed in.

God help me!

Marianne pulled up close to him, her berry flavored lips holding onto his thumb, was a sight so erotic, he knew they were in trouble if they stayed here. He would do something he shouldn't, and maybe frighten her. Imagining those sweet lips of hers wrapped around his cock instead of his thumb was too much to visualize and maintain decorum. He was on the edge already, hard and hungry for her. Darius had to suggest they return, before he lost his mind and took her right here on the sand.

CHAPTER 5

The Remembrance

Darius thought the weather perfect for their ride in the curricle. The clean scent of the June air mingled with the intoxicating fragrance of violets sitting beside him.

"Would you like to take the reins?" he offered.

"I would." She nodded. "You will help me?"

"Of course." Reaching one arm around her, he brought her close, transferring the reins into her hands. "Now grip firmly. Use the muscles in your forearms, not just your hands. Direct him. Tell the horse what you want from him."

As she followed his instructions, Darius buried his face in her neck, nuzzling his favorite spot. "He wants to please you."

"He must be a uniquely accommodating horse!" she sang at him.

She laughed a melodious sound. Her lovely laugh. It was a rare sound coming from her and he wanted to cherish the moment for the precious gift it was whenever he heard it.

"He pleases me. I wonder if I please him as much?"

"I can attest that you do with certainty, Marianne." It felt good to banter with her, the unspoken meaning of their words as clear as if they'd said them a loud. *She said you please her.*

They crossed over the ridge that looked down to the sea below. Darius put his hands over hers, assisting in slowing the curricle.

"This is a good place to get out. Walk with me?"

He reached up to grip around her slim waist, lifting her easily from the seat and down to the ground. Providing such service to her felt wonderful, as did the knowledge that it would be his "right" to do so for her always. He loved the feel of Marianne under his hands.

After securing the horse, he led her to the edge. He looked out.

"Right down there," he said, pointing, "is where I first remember seeing you." He met her eyes. "You were just a little girl, nine or ten years old. You were collecting fossil curies, and had them arranged in order from largest to smallest. I was with my dog, a great beast of a hound called Caesar. He was rampaging along the beach with boundless excitement, until he pelted through your careful array, scattering your collection. I saw all this happen from a distance. You jumped up fuming, soundly scolding him. Caesar was very repentant, and by the time I got to him, you were patting him on the head and saying, 'he was a good dog and probably didn't mean to be so stupid.' I tried to apologize for him. I said, 'I hope my dog wasn't a bother to you.' I remember that you repeated my words back to me. I've never forgotten. You looked up at me so solemnly and said, 'Your dog wasn't a bother to me, sir.' And then you sighed. You must have been very frustrated, but you were so composed and resolute, like a soldier."

"I remember the dog, and that day!" She looked at him in wonder. "That was you?"

He nodded. "I remember thinking what an intelligent, unspoiled child you were."

She blushed at his compliments, the rosy flush coloring her fair cheeks, making him want to press his lips to them and kiss over every inch.

"Mr. Simms used to pay a penny per five curies. He sold them in his shop to tourists. I thought myself very industrious, that it would make me a great fortune." She smiled, caught up in the remembering. "And Caesar? He is no longer with you?"

"No. He passed on after a full and happy life. But his

descendants are. You'll meet Brutus and Cleo soon—they'll be your very own personal guard." He paused before speaking softly. "That was the first time, Marianne."

She became quiet, almost as if she held her breath, waiting for him to say more.

"I remember the second time, too. It was maybe seven years later. You stood on that rock over there." Pointing toward the south end of the beach, he said, "The wind whipped your hair back and pressed your dress against your legs. You looked like you were waiting for something, standing there, perched on the rock, staring out to sea. I thought you so beautiful, and knew you were the same little girl. I recognized your hair, but it was your bearing and your manner, the way you carried yourself that was the same."

ALL this time?

Marianne could not have been more staggered by his revelations. How could he have been admiring her for so long?

"Darius, I had no idea." She could hardly believe what he'd told her and shook her head in denial. "I still don't comprehend why you would take an interest—"

"So, I left Somerset. Years passed, and I tried to forget

about you while I waited for you to grow up. Tried, but was not successful at all." He smiled, his thumb caressing under her eye. "It was impossible to forget you," he said very softly, his eyes boring into her.

"I–I am…"

"Shhh." He brought two fingers to her lips. "You don't have to say anything, Marianne. I just wanted you to know, that is all." Brightening, he said, "I have a gift for you."

"Another gift? You have given me so many, Darius."

"I want to give you gifts, Marianne. It pleases me to choose things for you."

"I have nothing to give to you," she told him, saddened by the thought.

"You're wrong. You give yourself—that is all I want." He nodded his assurance. "Come here." He turned her so her back leaned into his chest. He moved her hair aside, claiming her neck with his lips. "My favorite spot. I love to kiss you here on this part of your neck."

His warm skin, the manly scent of him, the weight of his body leaning into hers, felt good. He held her firmly, essentially trapping her in his embrace. She felt him grow hard below the waist, a ridge of iron pressing against her backside. So strong and wanting all at once. Marianne understood that Darius desired her, but for some reason, also apparently needed her. He needed her to be soft and submissive. And obedient. He needed her to be the soft dais upon which he could find some comfort. If she thought about it too much, it worried her, so she didn't. She turned the idea away. What if she let him down? Just like—

"Do you feel me?"

"Y…yes."

Oh, yes, I feel you.

"It's all because of you, Marianne. You do that to me. I get so hard for you, wanting you." He swept his lips up her neck. "Push back against me. Press your body to mine. You want to." Pulling her more firmly against him, he ground upward, slowly rocking his erection into her, all the while caressing her neck with his lips. "You make me happy, Marianne. So sweet, you smell like violets. Next to me like this, you are perfection."

She let the sensations float her. Wrapped in Darius's protective embrace, well-being enfolded her. The ridge at his hips felt huge pressing against her. Marianne was aware of the basic mechanics. She'd heard the stories and had friends who were already married. Darius would put that huge, hard piece of flesh into her. Would it hurt? It was said to hurt the first time. Would it bring pleasure? The sly comments and giggles of her married friends suggested it might. She knew it brought pleasure for the man, and was the only way to start a child growing. That husbands liked to do it often. That's what she'd been told by her friends at least.

Right now, the kissing and stroking of his tongue upon her neck gave her pleasure. Still, she was curious and wanted to know more. Darius did that to her. Made her willing to do things she had never dreamed of doing. She would have done anything he asked her to do in this moment. Marianne could not ever remember feeling so cherished.

"Your gift." He turned her and pulled out a box from his pocket. She opened the jeweler's box to see a choker of pearls, bearing a glowing crucifix pendant with a diamond center.

She snapped her face up to meet his. "Oh, Darius. It is so, so beautiful. I love it. A great many gifts you are giving to me. Such a generous man you are."

He was a great mystery to be solved. Why did he care so much, or at least treat her so? She didn't deserve all he was giving to her. Why on earth had he ever chosen her to be his? At times, it felt so overwhelming being the object of his desires.

"You will wear it for me, Marianne."

"I want to wear it for you, Darius."

And I do. I want to please you, so badly.

14th June, 1837

Today I learned something about Darius that shocked me. For years he has known of me. I remember him, too, as a young man, with his dog on the beach. He was polite to me even then. I am always left with the unending question of…why me? Suddenly, I am feeling more inclined to some sort of divine intervention in regards to Darius and his notice.

MG

CHAPTER 6

The Pleasure

His note arrived in the morning.

My beautiful Marianne,

I will send the carriage to collect you today at one o'clock. Wear your new riding outfit—the blue one. I have a surprise and await you eagerly.

D. R.

He greeted her with a kiss to her forehead and then pulled back to peruse her from head to toe.

"The color suits you, Marianne. You wear that blue very well."

"I haven't ridden in over a year."

"I'm sure it will all come back to you. Riding skill is not something one forgets. I just know you'll be splendid, but I am more than happy to help you if you need it." He seemed excited, smiling like a boy awaiting a treat, she thought.

She cried out when she saw her "surprise." The lovely gray horse standing in the stall was her own, Tempest. Or, at least she had been Marianne's horse before financial ruin had forced her sale. "Tempest?" Marianne petted her neck and leaned forward. "I can hardly believe she's real."

"For you, Marianne. She is yours once more."

Marianne whirled around to face him. "Darius? How did you know?" Her throat tight, she could hardly speak.

"Your father told me she had been sold to the Hallborough estate. Greymont is a good friend, and was happy to let her go. I bought her back is all." Darius looked at her questioningly. "Shall we ride?"

"Yes." Marianne would enjoy the thrill of riding again, it appeared. If she felt she could embrace the enjoyment she would tell him so, but she did not feel it would be honest.

They traversed inland, skirting over stones and grass until they reached a copse of trees. Darius announced it was a good place to stop and rest the horses. His strong arms reached for her and brought her down to stand on firm ground. He did not release her, but looked into her eyes. "What is bothering you?"

"Nothing," she said stiffly, knowing her answer would not be satisfactory to Darius. He would demand an explanation from her now. And she knew she would give it to him.

"Yes, there is something. You are melancholy, I can see it clear as day. Tell me." He rephrased it for her. "You want to tell me, Marianne."

Feeling a wash of relief fold over her, she lowered her gaze and whispered, "I–I don't deserve all of this." She shifted her eyes to rest upon Tempest. "It is too much, Darius. It makes me uncomfortable. I don't—"

"—I think you deserve it, and I'll help you get comfortable. Say to me, 'I deserve everything Darius gives me.' Say that, Marianne." His voice firm, harder than she had ever heard, commanded her. And she was helpless against his masterful directives.

"I...I deserve...everything Darius gives me."

"Yes, you do deserve *everything*, and now I'll make *sure* you're convinced." He took a blanket from the travel pack and spread it out on the ground. "I know what you need." He held out his hand to her. "Lie down with me, Marianne."

She carefully removed her hat before obeying. Marianne held on to his gaze as she lowered herself onto the blanket. Joining her, he stared down, his eyes raking over her, almost reverently, she thought. Darius certainly knew how to impel her, for it was easy to do his bidding.

She saw her eyes mirrored in his dark ones, the reflection easily visible as he descended. He began at her lips. Working leisurely, he used his teeth to scrape over her lips and tongue, gently grazing and sucking them into his mouth. He nipped along her jaw and under her chin. His hard body pressed into her side, then turned her to face him, seeking alignment from head to foot.

They fit against each other well, she thought.

After some time, he pulled back and stared again, focusing in on her face. No, it was above her face. He leaned down again and kissed her hair and inhaled. Whatever he asked of her, she knew she would do.

"Take your hair down for me."

She struggled to sit up, and he was quick to assist. Then he watched greedily as she removed the pins that held her hair. Darius sighed just before she plucked the last pivotal pin, her dark curls tumbling down in a curtain around her face. He looked happy watching.

Reaching out his hand, he lifted a curl and brought it to his nose. His face, so close she could feel the intake of breath drawing from her and into him. Warm lips came down on her almost desperately, seeking deep entry. His velvet tongue plumbed her as he pressed her back down on the blanket.

Fisting handfuls of her hair, he breathed in the scent, his weight settling back against her side. "I've imagined you like this with your glorious hair flowing free, lying in our bed, waiting for me." His mouth moved to her neck, grazing in the hollows with gentle lips and teeth. "Open the top of your dress. I want to see you, Marianne."

She did not hesitate. Her fingers moved quickly to tackle the neck cloth and unbutton her jacket. Darius helped. Pushing open her bodice, he was presented with the view of her breasts swelling above an alluring French silk corset. One that he had chosen for her. She knew he had thought of her wearing the garments against her skin. Darius had said. He also saw the pearls he'd given her, and froze. A ragged breath, and then another more controlled one expelled from him slowly, as if he needed to control his response.

"You wore them." Kissing over the tops of her breasts, he purred, exploring every uncovered inch, with wandering, but determined, lips. He even kissed the pearl crucifix framed below her throat. He had soft lips.

"*Bellissima*, so beautiful."

She liked his Italian words very much. When Darius said things to her in Italian, he sounded more intimate, and made her feel very adored. But his next move was bold, commandeering in its way. Cradling one hand behind her head, the other reached under her skirt and swept up her leg. She stiffened and shook her head. He just smiled and kept going, up to the top of her thigh. His hand moved inside, toward her sex. "Open up for me,

Marianne. You want this. You want me to touch you. Don't be afraid, *bella*. I want to feel you…and so, you want the same."

Sobbing out a moan, she obeyed, moving her legs apart. She quickly succumbed to tremors as his hand burned on her thigh.

"Your skin is so smooth, like the silk that covers you," he murmured.

Holding the back of her head, he forced her to look up at him. His long, elegant fingers journeyed on, burrowing in between more silk undergarments to the apex between her legs.

Oh God! He's going to touch me…there.

Her legs grew rigid, and she tried to close them, but Darius wouldn't allow it. His touch was firm as his determined fingers found her center and buried into the short curls that covered her cunny.

She sucked in a gasp at the feel of his hand plying her.

His fingers pressed a little harder, the pressure allowing her folds to part. That burning hot gate of entry he sought. It burned as hot as his eyes did, seeking complete surrender from her. One finger forged ahead of the others, pressing deeper still, and delved inside.

Marianne jerked hard when he invaded her, and groaned low in her throat. He was inside her body with his finger!

"Shhh," he whispered, holding her firmly. "It's all

right," he crooned at her lips, stroking into her slick cunny with his finger while hovering barely an inch from her face.

Marianne could not hold back the cry that escaped. Darius was so close and overriding she could do nothing but give in to him. But that was what they were both after, wasn't it? They each had their role to play. He would dominate. She would submit. In that way, both would be getting what they wanted, and needed.

Marianne's body responded in the only way it could.

When Darius felt her wetness, he arched his brows. "You're wet for me…and so soft." His lips brushed hers. "I knew you would be."

His words, so intimate, burned a path straight through her, laying her open, exposing her completely to his mercy. Arching sharply, her body arced and then froze as she accepted his invasion.

"That's it. Feel my touch in you. You're so soft here…and slick. I love that you're wet and slippery." His eyes flared before growing hooded. "God, you feel so perfectly lovely."

Dear, Lord! The things he said made her blush to the roots of her hair. But that did not curb her response to what he was doing to her. With a will all their own, her thighs clenched around his hand and her hips started to move.

Marianne couldn't keep still—the pleasure was

indescribable, setting her afire. Movement was as necessary as breathing.

Darius played her like an instrument, stroking over a swollen nub that shot bursts of sensation each time he drew over it. Slowly, he brought her to life, knowing where to touch and how hard to press. The hot pulses grew higher, more intense, building low in her belly. Nearly out of her mind, her neck straining, eyes closing, she thought she'd surely die if he stopped all that glorious rubbing. Something was happening to her. Maybe she *was* dying. She didn't care though—as long as he kept up stroking her in that most perfect, magnificent way.

"Look at me, Marianne. Don't close your eyes! Look at me!"

When he commanded her, something unraveled, breaking inside her. Her eyes began to flutter as the first convulsions struck. It was a struggle to keep them open, to obey his command. She tried to. Shudders of explosive current took hold, rushing throughout her body.

Darius stopped the rubbing and pressed the heel of his palm down hard. She felt her eyes welling, and then a single tear tumbled down each cheek as she stared up into his eyes.

The pleasure so powerful, she finally understood the craving Darius ignited in her body when he touched her. This was the culmination of the unearthly feelings he brought about. And it was…magnificent.

"Oh, Darius, you make me feel—" Shuddering into his neck, she panted and rode the wave, unable to finish her words.

"That was a glorious thing to watch, my beauty, you taking your pleasure. You *do* deserve everything. You deserve what I just gave you, Marianne, and there's so much more. I will show you everything." He pressed his lips to the streaks of tears on her cheeks, kissing the wetness away. He nodded slowly. "The next time you feel this same pleasure, it won't just be my fingers here against you." Pressing the heel of his hand against her mound, and his fingers atop her clit, he elicited an easy shiver and a moan. "It will be this." He took his hand away and mounted her, thrusting forcefully, his intent as unmistakable as the weight of him upon her.

Marianne felt every inch of his hard cock pulsing against her body, feeling him clearly through their clothes, his hips pushing her legs wider apart. His erection lay flat upon his belly and hit her right at the pubic bone. Instinctively, she offered resistance to his thrust, finding an immediate rhythm in the primeval stroking. He liked that *very* much, she could tell. *I like it very much.*

Smiling, he brought the fingers that had touched her to his mouth. She watched him put his lips around them and draw them back. When he pulled them out, he closed his eyes and said, "Like a spiced plum."

She gasped and clamped her eyes shut. The sight of

him tasting the fingers that had just been between her legs was so risqué she wanted to hide. It was as if he truly wanted to devour her. She turned her head away, embarrassment flushing her from the deep intimacy.

"No, no, no, my Marianne, we cannot have that." He took her chin and gently forced her right back to face him. "Do not turn from me. I will know *all* of you. I will, and that is my promise to you. How you look, how you feel, how you sound, how you smell, and even how you taste—I will experience them all, *bella*. Every beautiful part…of you…for me to know."

And Darius didn't release her right away after that either. He kept her close, on the blanket for a long time, holding and kissing and rocking against her body, whispering to her. Finally, when she was languid and calm in his arms, and Darius seemed satisfied that she had accepted his declaration—that she deserved everything he wanted to give her—he freed her. His words told her how he felt.

"Marianne, you are so perfect."

Darius, you are so wrong. I am nothing even close to perfect. I have done something unforgivable.

27th June, 1837

Darius made another gift to me today. He restored to me, my Tempest, who I adore. My horse is now my own again and I may ride when it suits me to do so. I love to have her with me once more, but the further I go into this tangled path with my future husband, the more troubled I become. I am so entangled with Darius in such a short time I know it must lead me into places that I am ignorant of. I look forward to him calling on me and spending time in his company.

He touched me today. Intimately. I know he has rights to do it, and even so it was bold of him, I could not deny his advances, nor would I wish to. His touch is demanding, but tender at the same time. He does not frighten me, but the place at which he is able to bring me—does. He says things, and kisses me, and touches me in ways that have brought me completely to his mercy. I am but mere clay in the hands of a master potter, and ever grateful he is so good with me.

MG

CHAPTER 7

The Marriage

Darius looked around the room and tried to settle himself in the moment as Marianne took up the pen and wrote her maiden name for the last time upon their marriage certificate. She looked as composed as she always did, so it was hard to judge what she felt. He knew what he felt though, and it involved just the two of them alone together in his bed.

Their wedding had been arranged as an elegant small affair with just family and a few friends. Marianne had asked Byrony to be her attendant, while Darius asked his cousin, Alexander Rourke, Lord Verlaine, to stand up for him. The Rothvales honored them as did the Carstones and others. Darius, being a respected member of the community, was bestowed with sincere congratulations and felicitations.

It was done. The vows had been given, the documents signed. Marianne belonged to him now, and the idea was a blessed relief. Now, if he could just get her alone and be rid of all these bothersome wedding guests. Well-wishes of family and friends aside, Darius wanted her all to himself, and found it a challenge to smile genially and to be patient.

"Mrs. Rourke, you are a vision of loveliness, and I find myself jealous of my cousin's good fortune," Alex complimented with admiration. "And I can see by the way he glares at me that Darius will be the possessive sort when it comes to you."

"Thank you for honoring us this day, Lord Verlaine." Marianne blushed as she thanked Alex, looking so very delectable Darius felt his mouth begin to water.

"Cousin, you are as astute as you are annoying, but correct as ever. My wife is loveliness personified, it's true, and I am possessive of her. I'll readily admit to both of your observations." He drew her hand up to his lips and kissed it reverently. "I cannot help any of it," he whispered while looking into her eyes, not caring who saw him.

"Apparently so, Darius." Alex chuckled wryly. "You read as an open book. But I am happy for you both and wish you all the best on your nuptials. You must bring yourselves to Orangewood soon, yes? When you desire for Town? I am sure Mrs. Rourke can find plenty of the London shops to her liking and she still must meet Gray. My brother sends his sincere regrets he could not come to celebrate the occasion of today." Alex bowed deep. "Look for an invitation and I'll not take no for an answer," he reminded as he took his leave.

Marianne embraced Byrony next. Promises of summer gatherings were made and accepted. Byrony's father, Lord Rothvale, offered his congratulations. "You are blessed, Rourke, and I wish both of you every happiness together. Now, when you can bear to leave your lovely bride for an hour or two, I want you to come and see me and we'll talk some more about getting you elected to Parliament. I know Verlaine can vouch for you, being family and all. You'd have the ready support of many. The Commons needs good men like you to take up the cause—"

"Yes, my darling," Lady Rothvale interrupted her husband with a smile and a gentle hand upon his arm. "I am sure Mr. Rourke has other things on his mind right now." She turned to Marianne. "My dear, you are a most beautiful bride, and the both of you make a stunning couple. I knew you two were meant for each other on the day of the strawberry picnic. I said it wouldn't be long before Marianne George got herself a new last name. Mr. Rourke had eyes only for you that day, and he still does. I daresay he made an excellent choice."

"Thank you for coming today, my lady," Marianne

answered, her face a mask of mysterious beauty, revealing nothing of her true feelings, yet suggesting their presence simmering just below the surface.

It drove Darius mad with desire for her. He wanted to know the woman beneath the quiet, graceful exterior. He couldn't wait to watch her face when she was lost to pleasure and coming undone in his arms as he made love to her, their skin melded together when he was buried inside her. *How much longer?*

"Thank you, my lady, I can only agree with you on the excellence of my choice," Darius answered politely, forcing himself to tamp down the lovely image of Marianne *in flagrante delicto* with him. All he could envision was her face as she lay on the blanket the day he'd taken her riding—the wild look, the surprise, the fire in her as she rode out that first climax under his fingers. He could remember how soft she had felt and would give just about anything to be back there right now. God, he was going to die right here in front of all these people, mad with lust for his beautiful bride! *How much longer?* Again, he shook off the visions creeping into his mind to attend to the guests in his home. Upon their departure, the Rothvales exacted a promise to attend them soon for dinner.

On and on the well-wishing went. They both kept smiling and thanking the guests for their attendance. All Darius really wanted was to pull Marianne into the closest room with a locking door and commence with the wedding night, but he couldn't do that of course. He had to maintain decorum and stand patiently by her luscious side, growing hungrier as the minutes ticked by.

Mr. George was the last to go. Mercifully he had maintained some sobriety for the occasion, but the haunted look in his eyes told Darius his new father-in-law would hit the bottle the second he was out the door.

With tears in his eyes, he faced his daughter. "You are the image of your mamma, lass. She would have been overjoyed this day." He took both of Marianne's hands, his whole body shaking. "Be happy, Marianne, with your husband. He'll care for you well." He looked to Darius and then back to Marianne. A wistful look came over him, and he seemed far away in his memories. "I just wish your mamma was here...and also your—" Mr. George cut himself off abruptly, attempting dignity for once, kissed her forehead, nodded to Darius, and made his escape.

The relief they both felt was palpable in the room. But Darius knew it was for very different reasons. Darius guessed Marianne felt relief knowing she had saved her father from ruin, and he was more than happy to give her that. Darius was relieved because his gamble had paid off—he'd gotten his prize. She belonged to him now. His dream was about to become reality.

DARIUS stopped them at the door after escorting her upstairs to the bedchamber. "I'll come to you in an hour. Your new maid will help you get ready," he said, his voice thick with suggestion.

Nodding in agreement, she couldn't help lowering her eyes. Understanding him precisely, Marianne knew why he was coming back and what she needed to be *ready* for. He had rights to her now, and he would definitely apply them without hesitation. Rights to take her to bed, make her his wife in every way.

"Look at me, Marianne." The command relieved her for some reason, and when she lifted her eyes she found Darius smiling down at her. "You've made me very happy. I just want you to know that. And you were such a gorgeous bride in your dress today. I am a fortunate man. You know, I'll no longer be just 'Mr. Rourke.' I imagine from now on there'll be an addendum whenever my name is mentioned. I'll forever be known as, 'Mr. Rourke, you know, that man with the beautiful wife.'"

"Oh, Darius," she whispered up to him, "that's a lovely compliment, but I don't think so."

He took both of her hands into his. "I absolutely *know* it is so. You are so lovely, and now you're mine." He leaned in to kiss her, a gentle brush of lips on lips, and then he swept them down to her palms, kissing first one, and then the other. "An hour, Marianne." He said it darkly, his eyes flashing, hovering over her hands. A moment later he was gone, leaving her alone to prepare herself for him.

Her new maid, Martha, was efficient in getting Marianne ready for Darius. Martha carefully helped her out of the palest blue silk gown Marianne had chosen for her wedding dress. As Martha took the elegant gown to put it away, Marianne thought about Darius. *My husband.*

After Martha left the room, Marianne had time to contemplate what would happen when Darius returned to claim her. Their encounter outdoors on the blanket a few days ago was still fresh in her mind. He'd touched and kissed much of her already. He'd given her pleasures, glorious feelings she wanted again, but frightened her, too.

Darius was going to do more with her tonight. He had made that fact very clear. This was their bargain though. He'd married her, and saved her father. In return he would have her body however he wanted, whenever he wanted. And she would have to submit to his demands.

Yes, submit to him.

Marianne was learning there was great pleasure to be had in submission. In granting that power to another. In giving herself to the person who commanded mastery over her. It was so simple. Freeing. The act of submitting freed her from her sin.

She expected Darius to be demanding—it was his way—but he never made her feel like she was doing anything distasteful. He was a mysterious and complicated man. Darius didn't just make her do things; he made her *want* to do them. And there was a very big difference in that.

Even so, Marianne's anxiety increased steadily until she was nearly quivering on the bed, waiting for her new husband to come and make her a woman. It wasn't fear of him really; it was more a fear of the unknown. The way he looked at her was overwhelming at times. So needful for a man. Powerful and needful—both, at the same time. It was the power Darius wielded in compelling her, mixed with that raging need of his, which was so entrammeling.

Help me to get through this…

STEPPING into the bedroom, Darius thrilled at the sight of his bride. She sat on her knees near the side of the bed, her hair down the way he loved it. She waited for him.

She's waiting for me to fuck her.

He could see that she trembled, and the sight pulled at his heart. As much as he desired her, Darius didn't care for her to be frightened. He wanted her to need him, not be afraid of him.

She lifted her eyes when she heard him come in. Their

gaze locked, and he could clearly see how unsettled she was. He wanted to rush over and gather her up. The urge to protect was strong, but as soon as he moved, Marianne bolted up from the bed, looking ready to run. He stopped and cocked an eyebrow. "Marianne?"

She answered him with nervous breaths. The thin silk of her nightdress rose and fell with the movement of her breasts as she breathed.

Godsblood, she was stunning! The need to get next to her, to know her, to take what was his, pounded at him. But he reminded himself he'd be careful. He had no intentions of ravaging her innocence. Darius knew she'd be soothed if he could touch her and get her into his arms. He started forward again.

She took a quick step back, her eyes flashing wildly now.

He froze at the sight of her panting.

She is *afraid.*

Realizing he'd frightened her sent a bolt of pain into his heart. Desire for her notwithstanding, Darius hated to scare her. He knew he had to tread carefully. He wasn't going to chase her around the room, for God's sake. Things just weren't going to be like that between them.

"Are you afraid of me, Marianne?"

She shook her head, but he wasn't convinced.

"Are you frightened of what will pass between us?"

A little gasp escaped, and then she turned her face

away.

"You were so beautiful sitting there on the bed waiting for me. I've longed for this moment with you for what feels like forever."

She grew very still, and he could tell she was listening to his words.

"You're my wife now, and I want to be with you. This is as it should be. Come to me, Marianne."

She snapped her eyes back to his.

"Walk to me, Marianne, to your husband. I want to hold you and kiss you. I've done that before, and it gave you pleasure. Remember? Don't you want to feel that pleasure again?"

"Yes," she whispered, barely audible.

"Then come here." He held out his arms, but didn't take a step. The victory would be in getting her to come to him. He thought he was close to his goal. She was wavering. "Come to me, *bella*." He waggled his fingers.

She took a step toward him.

He smiled at her. "You are so good, Marianne. You always do that which you are supposed to do, don't you?" He kept his arms out and his voice gentle as she took another tentative step.

She came forward.

"That's it, my beauty. Come into my arms."

He relished the view of her as she took slow steps toward him. The sway of her breasts brushing against the silk of her gown made his cock lurch. He wanted his mouth on her breasts. He wanted to see the perfection of them, feel the weight against his palm, to suck and lick and kiss them as he buried himself deep inside her.

When she got within the circle of his arms he drew her in. Her soft curves aligned along his body. Pure heaven. He breathed in the violet scent and held it.

She leaned her head into his chest and exhaled shakily.

Speaking softly, he said, "See how easy that was? And now here you are, in my arms, where you're supposed to be." He brought his hands around to cradle her face. "Look up at me. You want to. You'll see just how much I need you, my Marianne."

She lifted her face up to him. Seeing the blue of her eyes was an exhilarating sight—the perfect surrender to his command. Raw desire rolled off Darius like a crashing wave. He wondered if she could feel it emanating from every part of him. It was finally happening. She belonged to him now, and he could act on all of those things he'd dreamed of doing with her. No holding back. Not anymore.

Dipping his head to meet her lips, his hand moved to the back of her head, pulling her into him. The fire ignited the instant their lips touched, shaking Darius to the bone. The need to enter her screamed in his brain. *Get inside her body in some way. In any way.* His tongue pushed through her lips, mimicking the stroking his cock would soon be doing.

He ached for her terribly, ached to fill her up, to get in her deep and close. He'd told her what would happen before, and now he knew she waited for it. She'd become nervous and wary while she waited, and that was no good. He kissed her slowly and reverently, his tongue moving between her lips, urging her to flower open for him. Darius longed for Marianne, and the intensity of his desire nearly overpowered him. But he forced control of his raging lust. He needed to keep himself in check so as not to frighten her again. He was determined to initiate her carefully.

"Come here. Sit." He drew her to the bed and onto his lap, kissing deeply as he settled her into position. Her sweet, trembling warmth was intoxicating pressed against him. His cock was hard before, but now throbbed painfully under his robe. It was a challenge to hold back, but he forced himself to take it slow.

"Do you feel how hard I am? You do it to me," he breathed, rocking his cock up underneath her.

She whimpered in response, quivering in his arms.

"Shhh, you're all right. You feel so good on me." Gripping low on her back, he stroked through the silk nightgown. He felt her breaths increase to panting, matching her shaking.

"You're not afraid, Marianne. Not of me. I'd never hurt you. I will always protect and keep you safe. You know I only want you to be happy." He bent to graze at her neck, all the while keeping up the pressure of slowly grinding his cock into her. "I'm taking away your nightdress. I want to see all of you and kiss every part of your beautiful body. You want that don't you? Tell me that you do."

"Yessss."

"Say the words. I must hear the words come from your lips."

"I want you to kiss me…all over, Darius."

"Of course you do, sweet Marianne."

Darius found the hem of her gown, lifted it over her head, and tossed it away. He set her off his lap, taking in a deep breath.

God!

Marianne rested on bent elbows at her sides, her long legs crossed at the ankle. Darius could not speak—just wanted to touch and taste and see. Carnal, animal urges to crush her down on the sheets and fuck her wildly were controlled with effort.

Not this time. He couldn't hurt or terrify Marianne. She was too precious.

His hands started moving over her of their own free will. They cupped her breasts, lifting and drawing them together, learning their shape and weight.

"You're an angel, so beautiful and soft. You please me so much." He tweaked a nipple with two fingers and watched it pucker beautifully. "I want this in my mouth." Pressing her all the way down onto the bed, he whispered to her through kisses trailing over heated flesh and got his wish.

She moaned when he suckled her.

"Do you like my mouth on you?"

"Yessss."

He found and covered her other tight nipple, rolling the bud under his tongue, eliciting more soft cries out of her. Even so, she was still agitated and uneasy. He sensed anxiety from her and knew exactly what she needed.

"Marianne, I am going to help you. Let you feel safe while I make love to you. You want me to do it because it is what you need. I give you what you need, don't I?"

"Yes, you do, Darius."

"I am going to tie up your hands. You want me to tie up your hands. You want it because you know you'll like the way it makes you feel. You'll feel secure, Marianne."

Taking the silk sash from his robe, he secured her wrists together, above her head, to the bed. He was pleased to find the restraint had an immediate calming effect upon her. She lost the stiffness and softened under his hands. Feeling her ease into submission, he returned to pressing wet kisses to her straining breasts, sucking harder in places, marking them with love bites.

He dragged his tongue down further, burning a trail to her navel, where he explored with just the tip of his tongue pushed into the tiny opening. He felt her shiver in reaction. Sweeping on, he kept going to the place he desired above all others.

"Open your legs. I want to see you…and I want to taste you."

She flung her face to the side and shook it. "I cannot do that," she mumbled, shaking her head some more.

"Yes you can…and you will, Marianne." He turned her face from the side, forcing her to look at him once more. "Do it. Open."

He sat back and waited.

"You're going to be beautiful, and I want to see all of you."

The silence in the room grew thunderingly loud as he waited.

"Marianne, you want to do this. I know you do. You want to open yourself up for me. You will do it…for me."

She looked at him, and he saw it. He saw the expression in her eyes, and he knew. Darius knew the instant Marianne gave in to him—decided to submit and do his bidding. Darius felt his blood pounding in his head, his chest, and his cock. Everywhere. Nearly out of his blessed mind with desire for this woman, he waited for her to show him.

Her bound wrists thrust her breasts up, the nipples wound in tight buds. The weight of gravity pulled each mass slightly off center and to the sides of her rib cage. Darius stared, waiting, anticipating, dying. He felt the pounding blood thundering his heart in such magnitude his whole body moved with the beat of his essence. He sucked in a gulp of air.

She began to move. Slowly, Marianne bent first one knee and then the other. Her legs parted...

Oh, sweet Christ!

CHAPTER 8

The Plundering

Darius intended to devour her. This was the thought that flashed through Marianne's mind when she saw the look upon his face. He looked starved, ravenous even. Like he was hovering suspended, waiting for the moment he could begin on the sumptuous feast set out for him. She being his feast.

Marianne was splayed out on the bed with her hands above her head, tied with the sash from his robe. Her legs were bent at the knees and open for him because he'd told her to do it. If she thought too much on it, she got scared. So she didn't think—didn't even have the capacity to think about what she was doing right now. Darius would tell her what to do, and she would do it. And in that way, she could get through this experience.

His head hung between her thighs, poised to taste her cunny. Somehow she knew this was his intention. Then he paused and inhaled.

Oh, dear Lord! He was taking in her scent, aroused and blooming for him! The intimacy of how he attempted to consume her, simply made her burn hotter.

When he dipped down and pressed her folds apart like a butterfly, she twitched.

"Easy," he cooed, and then he unleashed his tongue. Licking, he made a single stroke over the sensitive skin at her slit, like he might draw cream off a spoon.

Marianne moaned at the ecstasy, the sounds coming out of her without volition. If she had known it would feel like this, resistance would have been the last thing on her mind.

He lifted his head and spoke to her. "Delicious. I want to remember this forever. Your innocent flavor as it is now...before I take you. So I may never forget how perfect you were in this moment."

Her eyes instantly filled with tears at his declaration. Darius might never want to forget her maiden flavor, but she would never forget those words. It was like he'd reached inside her and cradled her heart in his hands.

He dipped his head back down for more.

Yes, ohhhh yes, more please!

Darius swirled over every part of her sex except for the swollen nub at the center that cried out for some touching. Circling all around, he never brushed it with his tongue. He pushed two fingers just a little way inside, and her inner muscles instinctively clamped down on the penetration.

Slowly, he worked his fingers back and forth, all the while keeping with the stroking of his tongue. Marianne's response was to yield to him, to his tongue. God, she was his slave in this and thought she'd die if he stopped. Her cunny grew wetter and wetter, until she was drenched. She was ready to have him inside her. Ready to be taken.

He stopped, lifting his mouth away just a bit. "Do you feel pleasure, Marianne?" he asked, looking up at her. His mouth was shiny, his lips covered with her essence, glistening as he asked the question.

"Yes!"

"Do you want me? Inside you?"

"Yes!"

"Say it!"

"I want you! Please…inside me!"

He rewarded her. She understood that he was rewarding her for her obedience. He put his lips back down, onto her clit and kissed the spot, licking up and down.

She came. Her body tensed against the glorious, drawing suck he made upon her clit. The part of her capable of taking her to heaven.

"Dariussss!" She shouted out his name as the massive

climax took hold, controlling her, making her arch and buck against his fingers and tongue and lips. There was nothing left in the universe but the crashing shards of pleasure ripping through her and the magnificence he could create with his mouth.

HEARING Marianne crying out his name was a divine gift. The way her lips formed as they produced the sounds was indescribable in this moment of intimacy with her.

Darius wouldn't wait for her to ride out the orgasm though. He had to get inside her now, discover her, *know* her now, in this moment while she was climaxing.

His robe fell open as he crawled up to mount her. Darius set the blunt head of his cock to her hot, drenched flesh, thinking that this first contact felt so very right. The sensation of meeting her pussy to his prick stalled his breath.

Taking himself in hand, he rubbed the tip in her moisture first and then pushed until the head of him was inside and rested against a barrier. He knew what it was— her maidenhead. Sitting back on his knees, he cradled her from underneath, his big hands holding her steady. He lifted her towards him.

"Now, Marianne! Now I finally make you mine." Her

head rocked back at the same moment he drove into her untouched cove. There was a give in her body as he breached the barrier. Her soft cry pierced the silence, and his heart. He hated to hurt her.

Like a sword sliding into a scabbard, his cock settled into her as she accepted him inside.

Marianne was glorious.

"Ahhh...you're so good."

Her fluttering inner muscles gripped fiercely onto his shaft. The pleasure at being inside her finally was beyond his wildest imaginings. He held it in, giving her a chance to settle. Wet, tight quim clutched around his burning, iron-hard cock.

Unbelievable pleasure in her.

The need to kiss her overpowered the knowledge of exactly where he was in this moment. Dipping to take her lips, he covered her whole mouth with his and thrust his tongue in deep. She moved underneath him and made a sound. Just a small rolling undulation, and just the lightest moan, but in combination they worked as a signal. A gentle expression of submission and want, and he knew she was ready.

He pulled back slowly, deliciously, out of her cunny and her mouth, and then plunged back into both at once.

Yes, oh, yes, oh, yes...

That exquisite taste, once sampled, was impossible to hold back, and Darius let himself get lost in her. He thrust deeply but smoothly, relishing each slow, gliding stroke of his cock, knowing he was willing to explore forever that mesmerizing slit between her sweet thighs.

Being mindful of her innocence, he didn't want to take her too hard, but the urge to fuck overrode all sensibility.

I am not a monster, but I so want a proper fucking...oh, so very badly with her.

Sweet Christ, she was divine. Darius couldn't hold back what he was doing to her. In and out he stroked, hands working her hips against his strokes as the pace intensified. Dark moisture glistened on him when he pulled out—her virgin blood. The sight enflamed him even more, as did the knowledge he was the first and only to be inside her.

Watching each penetration spurred him to thrust faster. The head of his prick felt like it was going to burn off. The eruption was building, the need for completion too great to hold back any longer. Feeling his sac tighten in anticipation, he allowed the climax to consume him into oblivion.

"Mariannnnnne!" His essence jetted out the tip of him, pulsating wildly, washing her with his seed as he kept on stroking. He poured all of himself into her before slowing his rhythm and coming to a final rest.

My spunk is finally in you now, bella! Mine.

Time crashed down after that. Darius was not sure how long he floated in the sensation of extreme bliss at finally claiming her. She shifted beneath him.

"Oh, my beauty..." He rolled off to his side, stroking over her breasts, kissing her shoulder, her neck, and finally her lips. Releasing her hands, he drew her close, embracing her. *Mine.*

His gestures must have sparked something because she immediately began to cry, seeming totally overcome with sensitivity in the moment. She clung to him, pressing close, her face buried in his chest. *Mine.*

The two reactions were not what he expected, nor did they make any sense. She was clearly upset, but at the same time, trying to draw closer rather than to get away.

"*Mia cara*, my dear one?" he asked carefully, "did I hurt you very badly?"

"You did not." She sobbed through panting breaths.

"Frighten you?"

"No." More sobs shuddered through her.

"I am glad for that, but why do you cry?"

She shook her head.

"Tell me why, Marianne. You must tell me."

Her distress stabbed him straight in the heart. Darius didn't care for her crying. He wanted her happy, pleased, and content. He wanted her to feel pleasure, given by him. To be driven by his touch and to crave it. *Mine.*

He lowered his voice to the pitch she responded to so well and stroked her back. "You want to tell me, Marianne, and you will."

She buried her head further into his chest and heaved. "You—you make me burn like f—fire! I—did—not—know… it would be like this." She shuddered, her soft lips working against his skin as relief flooded him. *Perfection…just as I dreamed her.*

"Hmmm… But things are as they should be, my beauty." He turned toward her, cradling her face up to his with both hands so she could see him when he told her the rest. "It was my joy to show you. I adore making you burn." He kissed her softly, teasing her lips with his tongue. "I will continue to do it again and again because I know I cannot stop. You are too addicting, Marianne. And you make me burn like fire, just as hot." He kissed along her jaw and then her throat. "This is only the beginning, my bella. I have dreamed of you like this, discovering every part of you, *mia cara*—my dearest one."

"D-ariusss…" she breathed, her lips trembling, emotion clearly giving way to her usual reserve. He loved having her undone like this, naked and tangled with him, still flushed from her climax, soft and yielding against him.

So Darius showed Marianne again, and while he did, the same word continued to come to him as their bodies moved together. *Mine.*

CHAPTER 9

The Lesson

Darius woke in the night. The wind blew hard outside, rattling the trees against the house. Something wasn't right—she was not next to him in the bed. "Marianne?" He was unable to thwart the edge of panic escaping in his voice. Even he could hear it.

"I am here," her soft voice answered.

He followed the sound to the fireplace where she sat before the fire, hugging her knees. She had put her gown back on. The diaphanous thing trailed over the rug. Her long, dark curls rioted over her shoulders and down her back.

She looks like a goddess. And she is mine now. Truly mine.

He propped himself up on his elbows. "What are you doing down there?"

"Thinking."

"Of what, my darling?"

"Many things."

"Are you well, Marianne?"

She looked over at him then. Her eyes looked full of mystery and understanding at the same time. "Yes, Darius."

He shrugged into his robe before coming down to the rug, sitting back on his knees, facing her. For long minutes he stared, enjoying the view.

Gorgeous.

Marianne held his gaze and waited.

"You are so lovely. Your body is glorious. I want to see you. Take off your gown. You want to take it off for me, don't you?"

"I do," she answered.

He watched as she got to her knees and sat back before lifting the hem of her gown up over her head.

A woman of splendid form—that's what Marianne was. Breathtakingly fine. Delectable breasts with dusky rose nipples hardened immediately under his desiring gaze. They were marked all over with the feathery love bites he had made earlier. A flat stomach, slender waist, and the flare of lush hips framed the dark *V* of curls at the top of her thighs. That mysterious place he desired to know evermore. He wanted inside her again. No, he *had* to be inside her again!

Those eyes of hers, waiting…waiting…always waiting, looked to him for direction.

DARIUS opened his robe. His body was more beautiful than hers, Marianne thought. A beautiful man. Superb in physique. Smooth golden skin, rippled muscles on his lower chest and abdomen, the trail of dark hair that dipped low to encircle his cock. Sitting before her boldly, his shaft hard, needing her again, with no unease in his nudity, Darius wanted to take her again. Marianne knew all of this.

She thought about how it had been with him. Intimate, raging, tempestuous. He'd been inside her, pulsing and thrusting wildly, going deep. He'd filled her up with his seed and given sensations like she'd never known.

Once he'd told her she was beautiful when she took her pleasure and he'd loved watching it happen. She now understood what he'd meant. The beautiful part. Darius had looked beautiful to her when he had spilled inside her and found his release. His neck and arms rigid, looming over her, the weight of his hips, his eyes glowing down at her, his mouth working soundlessly before choking out her name. All of it beautiful to look upon.

Knowing she was giving him his pleasure was like a

drug, and it had affected her strangely. Marianne hadn't meant to cry like a baby, but when it was done, her emotions had bubbled up, overflowed, and out everything had come. She'd broken down and knew why. She felt guilty for having such joy. Surely this couldn't be fair for her to have so much. *Jonathan got nothing but death.*

Darius had been ever so sweet with her, though, holding and caressing. He was very good to her. He'd insisted on letting him cleanse her with a cool cloth. His hands so gentle, taking away the traces of her virginity and his seed. *I'm no longer a maid,* she thought, and felt great relief, glad the experience was behind her and not the ordeal she'd feared. Far from it. It was good. Being taken. It felt glorious with him.

Darius kept on staring at her boldly, his cock hard and jutting in her direction, looking like it wanted in her again...badly. Marianne wanted to touch it and kiss him there, in the way he had done for her, but she waited for him to tell her. His voice was everything. The words directed, but the pitch of his voice, the silky croon, bewitched her in totality.

"Touch me, Marianne. Put your hand around it and stroke up and down."

She leaned forward and wrapped her hand around his rigid cock. Her fingertips didn't quite meet her thumb though. She stroked up and down as he had told her, mesmerized by the velvety softness of the skin that sheathed him. The slit at the head opened up when she stroked downward and closed when she stroked upward. The opening and closing made a small sound because it was wet. A bit of shiny moisture wetted the slit. Marianne wanted to taste it, but she waited for him to tell her.

"Lick me. My cock, Marianne. You want to lick it and kiss it. Take it into your mouth and suck with those sweet, strawberry lips of yours."

She stretched down to meet his quivering cock flicking out her tongue, and licked the drop that seeped from the slit. He tasted salty but slightly sweet. She pointed her tongue and dipped inside the tiny hole for the remnants. She heard Darius groan above her. The sound of him made her hot all over. Even so, Marianne still waited for him to direct her.

"Take it all the way," he gasped.

The rigid flesh slid into her mouth, and she had to stretch her jaws wide to accommodate his girth, but relished the sensation of being filled. His scent carried the remains of what they'd done before…some of him and some of her mixed together.

Marianne realized it felt right to do this. She wanted to.

Descending slowly, she felt the head brush the back of her throat, and it spurred her on. Marianne liked his cock in her mouth.

Darius put his hands up to her head and buried them

in her hair, holding her mouth steady while slowly thrusting in and out, seeking a rhythm, just like before.

"God! You're magnificent. Your lips wrapped around my cock—ahhhhh."

Marianne kept working his flesh between her lips and would have continued, but he stilled their movements after a time. Gently holding her head still, he withdrew. She felt a bit of a loss when he left her mouth. Why did he want her to stop? She raised herself back up and flashed him a slight curl of a smile before licking her lips, rubbing them slowly together.

Darius brought his fingers to her lips, caressing, and told her why. "I don't want to come just yet. Sometime, I'd like to come in your mouth, but not this time," he whispered very softly.

Marianne smiled back at him, feeling suddenly bold. *He's mine.*

Yes, she would like to do that for him, remembering how exquisite his mouth had felt when he'd used it to pleasure her.

Darius came at her again, cupping the back of her head with one hand, and the other to cradle the base of her spine. He descended for a kiss. Marianne caught the lingering taste of him on her tongue as it blended with his own.

"Come here. Straddle my lap. Sit on me, my beauty."

She split her legs over the sides of his, folding them

under. His hot erection sandwiched up between her thighs, against her burning cunny, that ached for him again.

He guided himself, rubbing the head against her slick flesh. God, it felt divine when he did that. Whimpering, she pushed harder against him, seeking, needing, craving…

I just need it in me. Hard and deep and…now!

"You want my cock inside you again, Marianne? Tell me, my beauty!"

She did not hold back even an instant. "I want it inside me again, Darius!"

He served.

Twin, satisfied moans pierced the silence as he slid inside, filling her deeply.

"Ride me. Ride my cock!"

She gripped his shoulders and began to rock up and down his length. He cupped the cheeks of her bottom from below and helped.

Writhing atop him, Marianne thought she could not even care about what she looked like or be embarrassed by it. What they were doing was so shocking and pleasurable at the same time; she could die like this and surely wouldn't care. She wanted him hard and driving inside her. The feel of him piercing her through her own guiding movements was sublime, as was the knowledge that she was driving their sex this time. Up and down, she drew off and then dropped downward, encasing his cock, over and over and over.

Marianne was relieved to have Darius let her take him like this, as he wanted to do, and as she craved.

Her breasts swayed from all the movement, right before him. He captured first one nipple and then the other, sucking deeply, to the point of pain, pulling them up into his mouth. That sweet sting, mixed with the rasping of his cock teasing her clit, forced her to cry out in unimaginable pleasure.

They thrust together wildly. Back and forth, advance and retreat. She felt the spasms starting and bore down to squeeze tightly around him. Her shuddering cries must have told him she was climaxing, triggering an explosive release in him.

"Ahhh…ohhh…God, I'm going to come!"

She felt Darius get impossibly harder, just before he spurted his seed. It shot up deep, and she could smell the earthy scent she remembered from before.

He worked her fast, up and down, one last burst, his fingers gripping into the seam of her bottom. One final thrust finished the frenzy, and he crushed her to his chest, his cock jerking spasmodically.

He choked out roughly, "*Bellissima,* you are most splendid…"

Easing down from fulfillment, they stroked each other. Marianne rubbed his back and kissed his collarbone.

Darius kissed his favorite spot on her neck and caressed low on her hips. They stayed locked together for a long time.

Marianne felt his erection slowly soften inside her.

Eventually he roused them up to standing again. Helping her up, Darius kissed her deeply on the mouth and swept her into his arms, never breaking contact with her lips.

He carried her that way back to the bed, whispering through soft kisses the whole way. Cradling her head carefully, he laid her out, down on the bed. Darius was so gentle and tender in the way he touched her, it nearly caused her tears to return.

"Responding so sweetly to me, your skin touching mine is blissful, my Marianne."

Being drawn close, Marianne indulged in the comfort of his sculpted body next to hers.

They stared at one another, lying on their sides, eyes each studying the other's features. Marianne memorized every line, ridge, and hollow of his handsome face.

"I am glad, Darius, that I please you," she finally spoke, sighing into the security of his embrace, relishing the solace of being cherished. "I want to. It makes me feel…better. You know what I need."

He stroked over her hair. "I do know, Marianne, and I will always give you what you need. It is my duty to care for you and protect you now, and it gives me great pleasure to do so. Precious—that's what you are. You are precious and perfect to me."

Far, far from perfect, Darius!

1st July, 1837

I have learned of the pleasures of belonging to another in the most intimate ways between a man and a woman. He makes me burn when he touches me. The discovery of what passes between a husband and wife has been a revelation, and one I found very wonderful and beautiful. Darius is a perfect lover. Demanding, yet gentle with me, and done in a way that I adore. Darius always knows exactly what I need.

I trust him and want to be a good wife to him, but worry the day will come when I am not able to live up to his idea of me. My greatest fear is that Darius will become ashamed of me at some point, and I don't know how I will be able to bear his derision.

If it happens I don't know what I shall do. The loss of his affection would be the most painful for me to bear. He deserves the best of everything. I shall try to be all that Darius could ever want in a wife.

MR

CHAPTER 10

The Realization

Darius paused to look at Marianne, still sleeping in their bed. Her shining hair flowed out like a glossy halo upon the pillow. The sheet had slipped down, exposing one beauteous breast. Darius felt his breath catch at the sight of her. So beautiful. The stab to the gut that followed upon the heels of his admiration was so powerful, he widened his eyes at the sensation of pain. He wondered how unrecognizable he had truly become from the man he used to be. The past month had changed him. Marianne had changed him.

As the new mistress of a large estate, there had been much to acquaint her with. The house was named Stonewell Court, due to the light gray stone of which it was built, and stood along the southern coast. The sea could be viewed from the back of the house, which delighted Marianne. She'd told Darius so, and he didn't forget details like that.

There were an abundance of servants to introduce. Mr. and Mrs. West ran most business about the estate and house, Mr. West as Darius's steward, and Mrs. West as the housekeeper.

There were also the dogs. Darius had two wolfhounds, Brutus and Cleo, who took a great liking to their new mistress. If Marianne was outside, they were sure to be with her. When they were allowed inside the house, both were liable to be stretched out at her feet. Marianne told him she didn't mind. Darius had teased, saying she'd quite stolen away their loyalty to him, but secretly he was glad she did not mind the dogs, for their guard eased his worry some.

Upon this day though, Darius had business calling him away for the morning, and thus the reason for the stealth in observing his wife's womanly charms while she slept.

His breath caught at the sight, when she opened her eyes. So blue.

"Good morning, beautiful wife. I s'pose you've caught me leering at you before I must go." He reached out his knuckles to trace over the creamy, rounded flesh, her nipple hardening in response.

Catching his hand, she brought it to her lips. "You are leaving."

He nodded, loving the fact she'd kissed his hand. "Solicitors first, then some business with Greymont on a matter he's asked for some support."

"When will you return?"

He smiled at that. "Will you be missing me today, my sweet?"

She gave him the tiniest of nods and then a look.

"Did you want to say something, Marianne?"

"Yes."

"Tell me then. Say what you want me to know."

She hesitated before answering him. He could tell she struggled with her choice of words. "I am glad you stayed to wish me farewell. Please never leave me without a goodbye, Darius. I need that from you." She regarded him solemnly, her face a mask of intriguing beauty.

"Of course, my darling." He bent and kissed her lips, her neck, and finally her bared breast, covering the nipple and grazing with his teeth. "You taste so good," he moaned. When she arched into him he had half a mind to crawl back into the bed with her.

She did that to him. The need to have her was incessant. Morning, afternoon, night…didn't matter. The merest glimpse or gesture from her and he was lost. His cock was greedy when it came to Marianne. Darius wondered if his need for sex would ever abate. The more he had of her, the more he seemed to crave. And it wasn't the sex—it was *her* that drove him.

"What will you do today, Marianne?"

"I thought I might ride over to Papa's for a visit."

"Very well," he said quietly. "Please take the dogs with you, and don't stay too long. Remember we have dinner with the Rothvales tonight."

"I've not forgotten about it."

Darius was puzzled as he left though. Marianne had asked something of him for the first time. She never asked him for much of anything. He had to be extra vigilant to make sure she wasn't in need of something, for usually she would never ask on her own.

She was resolute about some things though. Marianne had continued to care for her father even after the wedding. She would go and keep company with him at her old house, a house which now belonged to him. Darius did not wholly approve, but he allowed her to do it. She was a dutiful daughter. Dutiful in all aspects as it was her nature. He sensed, and rightly so, that she needed to continue caring for her father. Being a dutiful son himself, he understood.

Darius tried to be an attentive husband. Frankly, he couldn't keep away from her for very long. He knew he was demanding of her. He couldn't keep his hands off her. The bedsport was magnificent, but it was Marianne's acceptance of him that was so sweetly given.

And every time was so good with her.

Desiring to have Marianne close, as well as to touch

her, all the time, was his typical response. He was hard pressed to keep away if she was within his reach, and it wasn't always for the sex. He sought the comfort of being intimate with her in any situation. Marianne's generous nature only made him want her more. And Darius knew why, too. He'd desired her for years, but now he knew his feelings were more than just desire. Much more.

He had fallen completely and utterly in love with his wife.

UPON his return, Darius hunted Marianne down. He found her in the library. She looked lovely standing at the window, reading a book in the light that the panes allowed in. At the sound of his steps, she turned. "You are back."

Darius nodded, leaning in the doorway, feeling wild, his cock flaring to life when she smiled at him, her blue eyes glittering, taking in the sight of him.

His breath grew heavy, moving his chest. His cock lengthened, struggling uncomfortably in his trousers. He bolted the door.

"You look fretful, Darius. Are you?"

He nodded again, stalking forward.

"Why are you fretful, Dar—"

He pounced. Like a wolf upon a rabbit, covering her

in possession. The book fell to the floor with a thud, echoing off the walls. Pinning her against the window, only one thought ran through his mind. *Because I need to fuck you.*

"Sorry, *bella*, I've thought of you all day, and I need to get my cock inside you right now."

"Ahhh, Darius!" She yelped as he picked her up and set her on the writing table.

His frank declaration served to fuel the need for her to unimaginable heights. Sweeping her skirts aside, he spread her wide before him, released his straining prick, and seated himself to the hilt. Looking down, he watched it disappear into the dark pink folds of her pussy. So hot. So stretched. So exquisite, his chest got tight from the knowledge. When he pulled out, his shaft shone, slick and wet from being inside her.

"God! You're so wet and ready for me!" That she was so responsive provoked him. "You're always like that, Marianne! God, it's so good—having—my—cock—in—side—you!" He punctuated each word with a thrusting stroke as he fucked into her. Hard.

He knew his wicked talk would incite her, too. Marianne liked it a little rough.

The sex pounded on, both of them lost to the cravings. His cock drilling into her tight grip, he felt her stiffen, readying herself for that delicious reward of the twisting coil of orgasm. Crying out his name as the sensations reverberated; she rode it out, looking wild and otherworldly in his arms.

Watching her come *was* a most beauteous thing, Darius thought. Seeing that moment of pure awareness in her expression was the fuse in bringing him to his own explosive release. Feeling her inner muscles squeeze tightly around his cock, he finally had to let go.

As he spilled out his release, he relished every spurt of spunk that washed into her, working it deep inside, sending it where it needed to go. He liked knowing she had his seed in her. He rationalized that it satisfied some primal male need to mate with her and produce his heirs. He wasn't sure if that was the reason, but regardless, he needed to put his seed in her, and the more of it the better.

MARIANNE did indeed thrill at his coarse words and the forceful sex. She loved the way Darius made her feel when he wanted her like this, like he needed her to live, to sustain his life. Like she was the only one who could satisfy his burning desires. At least that was how he made her feel. Even if it wasn't true, she would still embrace it for the pleasure it gave to him and to her.

Finally stopping, he came to a rest, covering her as she lay atop the table.

"Mia cara...ti amo." He whispered the words under his breath.

Despite his whispering, Marianne still heard him. She also knew what his words meant. Marianne was not fluent in Italian, but she knew he'd said, "I love you."

She stiffened underneath him and felt her newfound peace break apart like nest full of eggs hit with a stone.

Marianne waited for it. Waited for Darius to tell her to say it in return. She thought he might, but prayed he would not. She didn't think she could form the words from her mouth. Her heart thumped heavily in her chest and she felt the need for air.

Darius did not tell her to say it back. That command never came, and Marianne knew relief as the minutes wore on.

So, she did not offer the words back to him.

Powerful little words.

Marianne had to pause and wonder if Darius was aware of what he'd said to her. And if he was sincere, or rather succumbing to the passion of the moment. Marianne was finding that the sex had a way of breaking down reserve in the most powerful way.

At least for her it did.

The Passion of Darius

12th July, 1837

Today my husband said he loved me. He spoke his words in Italian, and in the heat of passion to leave me unsure if he was fully aware of what he said. I expected him to tell me to return the sentiment, but he never did. I am left with the incredible idea that he must feel more for me than he should. How is it possible for Darius to love me? How can that be? I know I shouldn't covet the idea, but I do...so very much.

MR

CHAPTER 11

The Ravishing

S o, my dear, have you kept up with your sketching?"
Lord Rothvale asked her at dinner.

"Yes, my lord. I try to put some time into it at least once per week," Marianne answered.

"Well, I've seen your work, and it's very good. Have you ever considered formal study?"

Marianne shook her head. "No, sir. Your Byrony is the real talent. Her portraits are so intuitive. She will know fame one day, I predict. For me, I just enjoy the sketching as a creative activity, and I only seem to want to paint the sea. It's the one subject I come back to over and over again."

Lord Rothvale gently patted her hand. "That's understandable, my dear," he said kindly. "When Mr.

Mallerton comes for his yearly holiday the two of you should collaborate. He enjoys seascapes as well."

"I would love to meet him, my lord. The great Mr. Mallerton, here in Somerset, working alongside me? I would be so enamored and dazed, I doubt I would be able to speak, let alone draw anything." Marianne couldn't imagine the scenario, but would be so honored to meet the great master himself. Lord Rothvale and Tristan Mallerton had gone to school together and were the best of friends. Moments like these made her wonder if she was indeed dreaming.

Lady Rothvale spoke up, "Marianne, darling, you should have your portrait painted by Mr. Mallerton when he is here. Don't you agree, Mr. Rourke?"

"I shall inquire for one myself, my lady. There is nothing I would love more than a portrait of my wife," Darius replied smoothly. He probably would commission a portrait of her, Marianne thought. The very idea was almost too much to consider, but she knew her husband well enough already to know he would do what he wished on the matter.

Lord Rothvale directed his next comment to Darius. "What do you think of your wife's artistic talent there, Rourke?"

"Well, I think she's quite accomplished, and I love to watch her at work. The concentration, the furrowed brow, the intensity with which she studies the seascape is fascinating. She's very hard on herself, though. Never pleased with what she's drawn when to my eye it looks good enough for your National Gallery," Darius said.

Lord Rothvale chuckled. "Getting that thing founded will be my life's work, I suppose, and much harder than it ought to be, but then, worthwhile endeavors usually are. We'll make sure to leave a nice wall for her." He winked at Marianne. "Now if I can just get your husband to consider public service, I imagine how much good could be accomplished with men like him in Parliament. What do you say, Rourke? Make a run for the constituency at Kilve?"

"I'm thinking about it, my lord," Darius told him, but he looked at Marianne. There was hunger in his eyes. Marianne knew he wasn't thinking about politics right now. He was thinking about what he wanted to do to her when he got her all to himself.

THE staring only got worse on the ride home. Darius sat opposite her in the carriage, his eyes roaming over her body in a ravenous sweep that left no doubts about what was on his mind. She shivered in anticipation, feeling herself go wet between the thighs. Apparently their frantic session in the library before dinner had only whet his appetite for a more leisurely paced encounter tonight.

"Come to my room this time," he whispered in her ear when he escorted her up to her chamber. "I'll be waiting for you, my beauty…and don't bother wearing much." He bore the grin of a devil. A very handsome, but lascivious devil.

Marianne chose one of her new French nightgowns, a Madame Trulier specialty. Very scant, sleeveless silk in ice-blue, low cut and close fitting so every curve was emphasized. He'd said not to wear much, and to her eye it certainly qualified. It was a moot point though, because she wouldn't have it on for long. Darius would have her naked in a heartbeat.

Pushing open the door to the master's chamber, she felt the muscles in her abdomen clench and the need for air into her lungs increase. His effect on her was consistent. It wasn't fear for he never hurt her, but he did rattle her—most thoroughly. When Darius wanted her, she got nervous. Not because she didn't want the intimacy, but because she did. He was a very skilled lover, taking her body to places she could never have imagined, and made her lose herself in exquisite sensations of pleasure and wantonness so intense that it was a little frightening. The anticipation of what was waiting never failed to make her skittish. And she knew something else, too. Darius liked her a little skittish in the beginning so he could woo her and enjoy her submission when he brought her to ecstasy.

The room was dim, and she didn't see him anywhere in it. He wasn't in the enormous bed, and he wasn't by the hearth. She thought it odd that she could have beaten him in preparing for bed. Darius was always the one willing, ready, and waiting on her.

Sighing, she walked to the balcony doors and went outside. The summer air was warm, and the stars shone clear. It was a beautiful night, and she could smell honeysuckle wafting up to her from the vines below. The sweet scent reminded Marianne of her mother.

Now that she was married, Marianne wondered about her own parents. Had they shared the kind of passion Marianne had in her own marriage? She smiled and shook her head. Hard to imagine. Nothing had really prepared her for the intimacy of sex. Being so close with Darius physically, had quickly broken down her emotional walls. Aloofness was impossible when another person was inside your body and making you cry from the pleasures they gave you.

Marianne went back inside to wait. As soon as she stepped through the balcony doors strong arms enfolded her from behind, trapping her securely against a hard, muscular chest. And more than just his chest was hard, too. She could feel every inch of the long, thick length of his cock pressing against her bottom. Marianne couldn't see Darius because he was behind her, but he was definitely naked, definitely aroused, and definitely intent on having her.

"Darius," she gasped, "you surprised me."

He nuzzled her neck, warm lips lingering over her pulse, his teeth nipping gently. Big hands drew up and down her bare arms, slowly and possessively. "You surprised *me* standing out there in this gown, looking like an angel. I was speechless, so I just watched you and thought about what I'd do when you came back inside..."

"What are you going to do?" She panted against him, her body heating up from the press of his erection and the whisper of his voice.

"Do you trust me, Marianne?" He swept his hands up her sides, over her ribs, and stopped just under her breasts.

The anticipation of his hands so close, but not touching, made her arch into him in an attempt to meet the distance. "Yes, I do, Darius."

"Good girl." His hands engulfed both breasts and squeezed. Her nipples budded up hard and tight, and he tweaked them through the thin silk. Sparks of pure pleasure pricked her skin, and she had to swallow the cry on her lips, knowing this was her reward for entrusting her pleasure to him. "Keep trusting me, Marianne. Trust me...and just feel."

Marianne shivered, wondering what he would do. It was always the anticipation that got to her. Darius knew how to arouse her until she could do nothing or want nothing but what he could give her. He made her needful.

"I will. I do," she whispered. And then he draped a silk sash in front of her face and lowered it onto her eyes. He tied it in a knot. Her blindfold was secure, and she could see nothing. *Just feel. That's what I am going to do.*

DARIUS stepped back and admired from behind. The scanty gown she wore was lovely, but it was time for it to go. He bent, took the hem in his hands, and drew it up, over her head and off. He sighed in contentment. Naked at last. He knew what he did was scandalous but couldn't imagine having Marianne any other way. Making love with her fumbling in nightclothes in the dark would be a travesty. That luscious body was meant to be devoured with his eyes when he took her.

He cupped the twin globes of her arse, lifting and forcing her to spread her legs a little. "Such a pretty arse you have, so round and smooth." He squeezed each cheek from the bottom, the fingers of both hands meeting at her cleft and the slippery wet that drenched it.

She shuddered when he fingered her quim and moaned a little in that breathy, sexy way. God, when she made that sound it drove him wild, gave him crazy impulses, turned him into a sexual fiend. The need to penetrate her body shouted from inside his brain.

"I love that you're wet for me. Soon, my beauty, soon, I'll be driving inside your sleek, wet quim and making you scream. And then I'll do it over and over again. All night long until the sun comes up." She whimpered in protest when he took his fingers away. "Walk for me first. I want to see that beauteous arse. Go on. Take about ten steps straight forward and you'll get to the side of the bed."

She took a tentative step, and then another, and another. She walked her pretty arse over to the edge of the bed and stopped. He groaned from the sight of her muscles flexing and shifting as her long legs moved across the distance. She turned to him even though he knew she couldn't see him through the blindfold.

"What do you want, Marianne?" he asked.

"I want you." She trembled with need, her breasts vibrating, her nipples hard and peaked.

"How do you want me, my beauty?"

"Inside me. I want your cock inside me."

Her pleading voice flipped something in his brain. Any control he had maintained throughout the evening simply evaporated all in an instant. He was on her before he could suck in another breath, his hands pushing her torso down on the bed and then gripping to frame her hips. Going at her from behind this way made his cock jerk, like a leaping stallion trying to mount a mare. He became a beast of sorts, wicked and decadent and primal.

Marianne's breaths were labored as he split her legs

further apart. He could smell her tangy essence blooming for him, wet and hot and ready to receive him. Guiding his cock to her entrance, he sheathed himself to his bollocks in one claiming stroke. The sweet, tight grip of her cunny was so good he thought it a kind of pain, but one he could seek again and again and again. Her heavy breaths stopped when he impaled her, in shock most likely, but she took him all the way to the root without complaint, and then ground back as if she could take even more.

She's so damned perfect!

He had her hard. No doubt about it—this was a hard fucking. But right now, he needed it. Later he could be gentle and slow, but first he had to feed the beast in him. There was only one thing on the menu for the beast, and it was sweet and pink and situated right between Marianne's thighs. He could get inside her deeper in this position than in any of the other ways. Oh, fucking hellfire, he thought, please never let it end!

Pumping fiercely, he ground into her like a madman, time slipping away behind a veil of carnal sensation. He had no idea how long he fucked, if it was a second, a minute or an hour, who knew?

He reached down a finger to glide over her clit, and the second he did, she came, all at once, clenching and shuddering beneath him. Her orgasm ignited his own release. It was nirvana to pleasure her, to feel her body tense up, to hear her cries. He felt his own need bubble up and overflow like wine from a cask. Her glorious response pushed him over the edge where he could embrace the end he sought so desperately. With a shout and a hiss and a gush of hot seed he melded into her and, for one brilliant instant, knew absolute heaven.

About an hour later she was languid and sleepy in his arms—a well-ridden, thoroughly sated, and stunningly sensual woman. Her blindfold long removed, she had crawled up on him, her head at his chest where she kissed and trailed her sweet lips up to his jaw and his shoulders.

He thought about all that he had known about her before and all that he knew about her now. Darius was happy to realize he'd been correct in predicting the passion in her. His Marianne was a siren in bed. She was also affectionate, and he adored her touches and gestures. After they made love like this, he liked to hold her close against his body, kissing and stroking over her skin. Whenever she did the same to him, his heart swelled. Marianne made him feel victorious, like a warrior, strong and powerful. But there were many facets to her, and in some ways she was more of a mystery now than before. He sensed a kind of darkness in Marianne and that was a concern. Darius knew his feelings for her were growing stronger with each passing day, and with those feelings, the urge to protect and secure her happiness however he could.

"*Cara*, why did you seem sad when Lord Rothvale asked you about your drawings?"

"Did I?"

"Yes. To me you did. And he even patted your hand to console you a little, it looked like. Why does drawing the sea make you melancholy?"

She sucked in a quick breath before answering. "I think it's because the sea is so demanding."

"Demanding?" Her explanation struck him as odd. "In what way?"

"No matter where I go, the sea calls to me, and it has for a long time. I cannot get away from the pull of the waves, and I fear it will always be so. Somehow, capturing one moment of time depicted in a seascape is soothing for me. That's why I only draw the—" She shook her head and looked at him. "Enough about that. I want to talk about you. Lord Rothvale is serious about you making a run for the House of Commons, and I think he is right. You would be very good, Darius…"

He smiled and kissed the top of her head, thinking about how she'd just avoided his questions so neatly. Marianne was loving and kind and attentive. He could not fault her as a wife in regards to how she embraced her many duties and responded to him. And he believed her sincere. So why then was there this persistent nag in the back of his mind telling him that Marianne wasn't being completely honest?

13th July, 1837

   Darius is getting closer to my secret. He wanted to know why I seemed melancholy when Lord Rothvale asked me the question about my drawing. How can I tell him the truth? And if I do, will his good opinion of me be lost? I cannot bear the idea. It hurts me too greatly to contemplate. I need his cherishing too much.

MR

CHAPTER 12

The Gift

A week passed before he said it again.

Marianne searched in all of the usual places. She'd come to her study to review the housekeeping accounts, but the books weren't here. Her desk had been rearranged as well. Very odd. She would inquire to Mrs. West and get to the bottom of the mystery. Shuffling through another drawer in her quest, she didn't hear him come in.

"Looking for something, my darling?"

"Oh, Darius. Yes, actually. I came up here to review the accounts, but I cannot find the housekeeping books. They are nowhere in this room that I can see, and someone's been fumbling around my desk."

"Well that's no good at all. We must find the culprit

and see to a swift punishment." He walked over and pulled her up.

Marianne knew he was up to something as soon as he started in on the teasing. She could smell it on him.

"What do you know, Darius?"

"Only that your neck flushes when you get frustrated." He smirked. "And you get a little crease, right here, between your eyes." He brushed the place with his lips.

"Well, yes I'm frustrated—I cannot find the books!"

"Oh, I'm sure they'll turn up, Marianne. Probably sooner than you think. These things have a way of working out." He waved a hand in dismissal.

She observed him carefully. He looked very smug and rather devious. "Did you want…something, Darius? You know, when you came in here?"

"I s'pose a kiss would be nice, but that's not why I came to find you. Actually I am in need of your opinion on something. Will you come and let me show you?" He held out his hand, a definite leer of mischievousness above that firm jaw.

She took his offered hand and let him lead her down the corridor and into the south wing of the house. He stopped them at a door near the end of the hall.

"What I want you to see is in here." He smiled knowingly. "Now close your eyes."

"Another surprise? Don't you get tired of surprising me, Darius?" She eyed him warily.

"Never. Now be a good girl and close your eyes," he growled.

She obeyed because it was what she did when he gave her an order. She closed her eyes and heard him open the door. He brought her into the room.

"You may open your eyes now, my darling."

She looked around the elegant room and fell in love. It faced south and had a picture window with a view of the sea framed in one wall. A lady's desk was arranged afore the window, for light. There were upholstered chairs in a turquoise silk and a large chaise set before the fireplace. The earthy colors of blue, green, and the dark brown woods appealed to her. The thick carpet was warm and luxurious. This was an absolutely flawless room.

"What is this place?"

He didn't answer as she walked over to the desk. She put her hands on the English oak and splayed out her fingers. What a magnificent working desk, she thought. You could sit at this desk and view the sea anytime you wished. How pleasant it would be to relax in a room such as this.

"Sit down, Marianne."

She pulled out the chair and sat. She looked out the window. The day was gusty, the choppy whitecaps bobbing for miles. A lone merchant vessel sailed by

"Open the middle drawer."

The drawer contained engraved stationary for

correspondence. Lifting a sheet of the heavy linen paper, she read the engraving, Mrs. Marianne Rourke, Stonewell Court, Kilve, Somerset. A breathy laugh escaped and she brought her other hand up to her mouth to muffle the sound. She could feel Darius had moved. He was directly behind her.

"Now open the bottom, right drawer."

The sound of wood sliding against wood squeaked harshly in the quiet between them. The account books. Her housekeeping books were stacked neatly and ordered just as they should be in the drawer.

"Oh…Darius…"

"Do you like your new study, Marianne?"

She leapt up and spun around. He was right there before her, smiling broadly.

"Like it? No. 'Like' is an unsuitable word for how I feel about this room. Darius, I *love* this room!"

She leaned up to kiss him on the lips. She put a hand to his cheek and asked, "Why?"

He shrugged. "I know how much you like the views and thought you deserved a nice place for your work. A beautiful place for a beautiful woman." He turned his lips to kiss her palm still resting on his cheek.

"Thank you," she whispered.

Deserved. There was that word again. He said she deserved this room, but really she didn't. Would he still think her deserving if he knew? Still, she wouldn't hurt his feelings. She'd accept his lovely gift and show Darius her appreciation as a dutiful wife should.

"You might even be able to sketch up here, the light is good. Anyway, I'm glad you're happy with it."

"I am, Darius. Very much so." She embraced him and felt his strong arms wrap around her.

The knock at the door alerted them that the tea had arrived. Both pulled out of their embrace at the same time. Sitting side by side on the chaise they watched quietly as the maid set out the tea for them. Marianne looked at Darius, so dignified and handsome as he waited for the maid to finish and leave them alone again.

Darius picked up a strawberry from the plate and held it to her lips. "Open your mouth and bite." His eyes awaited, looking covetous and hungry now.

She covered the berry and closed her teeth over it. Juice squirted around her tongue, the tangy sweet perfume releasing into the air. She chewed the soft fruit and swallowed slowly, never taking her eyes off him.

He lunged and was on her in an instant. His tongue pushed deep and swirled over every inch of her mouth, sweeping up traces of the lingering strawberry flavor.

She felt herself go instantly wet for him. The heat flooded her between the thighs, and she had to clench them together for relief.

He pulled back, arched his brow, and stared.

She stared back.

He touched her forehead gently.

"What do you think about in that mind of yours, Marianne? So many thoughts you must have. When you look like you do right now…I wish I knew what you were thinking."

"Right now I'm thinking I want to do something…for you, Darius."

His nostrils flared and his eyes widened. "What do you want to do for me?" he whispered with controlled breath.

She moved from the chaise and knelt on her knees before him. Lifting her face, she pierced him with her eyes and rubbed her lips together.

Darius opened his mouth in surprise, but no sound came forth. He was a tight as a bowstring and ready to snap, but choked out the command. "Tell me what you want to do. Say the words."

She was relentlessly frank with him. "I want to suck your cock, Darius."

A kind of whimper came out of him, and she liked the sound he made. She moved her fingers quickly, releasing the buttons that covered him. His cock sprang out proud and hot in her hands. Gripping at the base with one hand, she lowered her mouth. Her tongue licked at the tip. She could smell his musky male scent. He jerked sharply and then arched into her touch as she closed over the bell end and pushed him to the back of her throat.

Darius moaned and strained under her onslaught. His

harsh breathing just about matched the pace of her sliding strokes. He gripped her head and pumped into her mouth. And she liked every bit of what he did. From the first, Marianne had found pleasuring him with her mouth to be exciting—never unpleasant. He did the same for her, and she loved that, too. He gave her orgasms when he put his tongue to her. But Darius had never allowed her to finish him with her mouth. She wanted to know what it was like when he exploded in passion and her tongue was around him.

She could tell he was close and doubled her efforts of sucking as he slid in and out. She enfolded his bollocks in her free hand and squeezed the tightening sac. All in a rush it happened. She felt the burst under her hand and heard the gasping above her head. A warm gush filled her mouth, and she held it as he convulsed into her throat, feeling victorious, and strangely happy.

When she pulled back from him they shared another look. He stared at her mouth. She slowly swallowed the salty tang and smiled at him. His face broke in an expression of near pain, and he answered her in a rush of sentiment, spoken in Italian, the words harmonious and flowing, but nevertheless unknown to her.

Darius recovered quickly, restored his clothing, swept her up into his arms, and marched her all the way to their bedroom. Marianne's clothes were stripped from her body the instant the bolt was thrown. He plucked out her hairpins, buried his hands in her hair, and was inside her before she could blink.

He became a ravening beast who took her wildly, looming over her, his driving hips splitting her thighs as wide as they could go. He suckled her hard, too, leaving fresh love bites on her back when he flipped her and took her from behind, plundering her deep and furious.

After that wild session, he settled down and slowed the pace. Languid and unhurried, he lapped at her cunny, tasting her, teasing her clit, making her climax again and again. He whispered more words to her in Italian. She still didn't understand the meaning but found the sound of them to be very wonderful indeed.

"Your Italian words are beautiful, Darius. Why Italian?"

He looked surprised. "You do not know about my mother?"

She raised her eyes to his. "Your mother was Italian, then? I've wondered. You've a darker complexion than most Englishmen." Touching his hair, she smoothed it back over his brow, appreciating what a handsome man he was. "Did she die when you were a boy?"

"She's not dead. My mother lives, just not in England. Rome is where she resides, as she has done for many years. She named me. Darius is a Roman name."

"I had no idea. Do you visit her?"

"Yes. I am a dutiful son." Shifting against her, he

settled her head firmly underneath his jaw, stroking over his favorite spot on her neck.

She caressed his chest as she lay against him. When he spoke, his voice was different. Marianne sensed sadness and regret in him. "My mother is a cold sort of woman. Sometime we will go to Rome, and you will meet her. It is no large matter though. I no longer seek her favor." He turned his face so she couldn't see his eyes. "My father met her on his tour of Europe and brought her here after they married. She was unhappy and resented me, I think, because with a child to raise, she could not leave him and return to her homeland. There were no more children between them, but she stayed until I left for school— probably to assuage her guilt. My father made certain I saw my mother for regular visits."

Marianne's heart ached for Darius. She pictured him as a lonely little boy seeking his mother's love and finding the cold boundaries of duty instead. "She was not a proper mother to you." Marianne frowned, thinking she would find it hard to be courteous to her mother-in-law upon such a time as she might meet her.

"She was proper, just not very demonstrative. I wanted her to love me, but I don't believe she was able to show it outright. In her heart, she is too constrained." He kissed her hair. "You are nothing like her, Marianne."

"I do not want to be like her. I would show my children love because that is what a mother is supposed to do. Children are a precious gift, to be cherished and…protected."

"Do you want to be a mother?"

"Of course I do, Darius." *But I don't deserve to be one.*

"Tell me. Tell me you will want my child, please. I need to hear that from you, Marianne."

He sounded almost desperate. The overwhelming urge to soothe and reassure him was necessary. Something she had to do. "I want your child, Darius. I do, truly." She kissed him on his chest, feeling him relax. It was a small kind of comfort in knowing he wanted her in that way, that that her answer eased him.

"I am so glad. You will be a wonderful mother to our children."

How could I ever be?

"What of your father?" She moved from his embrace so she could see his face.

He smiled fondly. "Father tried to make up for her. He was excellent. I was but five and twenty when he died," he said wistfully.

"I do remember him, vaguely, at church." She touched his cheek. "You look like him, from what I remember, and the portraits in the house. Very handsome, the both of you."

Her compliment seemed to affect him, and she sensed melancholy and regret in him. It saddened her.

"I wish he could have known you as mine."

"I do as well, Darius."

Very softly he said, "I think you perfect, Marianne." He met her lips in a deep kiss. "*Ti amo.*" He whispered it so quietly she might not have heard. But she did hear.

Again, she stilled.

Oh, Darius, you should not love me!

Marianne felt sick to her stomach, and guilty, like she had bewitched him with dishonesty. And she knew if he was aware of the truth about her, he would regret his declaration. But the selfish part of her waited for Darius to tell her to say the words back to him. The silence hung heavy as she waited for it.

He didn't. And the selfish part of her wanted him to command her to say she loved him. She wondered why he didn't, and frowned. He had asked her to tell him she wanted his children. Why not this?

Marianne got quiet then, and still, contemplating until she accepted the reason. Darius did not want her to say it. If there was one thing she knew about Darius, it was that he acted on his desires. He knew what he wanted and had no trouble voicing or demanding it. So then, that left only one possibility. He didn't want love from her. He wanted her body and her companionship and her obedience to him. As it should be...

The Passion of Darius

THE first time he'd said those words he was hardly aware, so often it swirled in his thoughts. This time, however, Darius was fully conscious his declaration was not returned, and the pain of that knowledge was excruciating. He'd observed her frown and felt her stiffen up, and that had hurt even more.

The thing that attracted him to her in the first place— her submissiveness—had also trapped him. He could tell her to do things, say words, and think thoughts, and she would, but he could not tell her to say that she loved him. He physically could not. Because if he did that, then he might never know if she only said the words to please him. Maybe he would never know the truth, but he simply could not bear for her to tell him she loved him when in fact she didn't. Just couldn't endure the thought of it. He vowed he'd refrain from voicing the sentiment aloud to her again.

CHAPTER 13

The Grief

The two of them went along together in this way for many weeks, until Marianne's father died. Mr. George aspirated his own vomit while passed out from too much drink. Darius was the one to tell her and to hold her while she cried her heart out. Grateful Marianne was spared the burden of discovering her father dead, he took consolation in that small blessing at least. That dubious "honor" had gone to Mr. George's housekeeper instead, who'd found him cold and already stiff in the bed.

Marianne grieved, of course, the last member of her family dead, and under sad circumstances. Darius agonized for Marianne, wishing he could ease her pain. For all that he had disapproved of Mr. George, he was still his wife's father and loved by her. She had shared fond memories of him from childhood.

The sight of her mourning at the graves of her parents rent his heart. So sorrowfully beautiful, dressed completely in jet black, the only points of color being her blue eyes and the pearl crucifix he'd given her, would be an image of Marianne he'd never forget.

Darius could see that Marianne missed her father, and he began to worry. He worried that Marianne did not have cause to need him anymore. It was not necessary to be reminded of how he'd won her. She had sacrificed herself to save her father. Darius knew that. Well, her father no longer needed saving. He was dead. And because of that, Marianne did not really need Darius any longer.

She might not need him, but she was stuck with him, for he would never let her go. The very idea was an impossibility. She was his precious Marianne, whom he loved more than anything. The wife he loved, even though she clearly didn't love him in return.

Loving was never part of the plan, but in matters of the heart, things rarely go to plan. It was simple, really. He loved Marianne and had told her so. Hearing the sentiment returned was his greatest wish. On more than one occasion he had told her, and the pain of the absence of those words given back was acute.

Darius didn't know what he could do about it though.

He'd made such a mess of everything and was now so entangled, he felt like a puppet bounced along on a string.

There was also the idea Marianne might be pregnant. They'd made love nearly every day, and she had never been indisposed to him. Not once. The fear that she could resent being tied to him was reminiscent of his own parents. He fervently prayed she would welcome a child. Marianne would be a loving mother, he thought, nothing like his own. 'Twas part of why he'd chosen her…

After the funeral, Marianne started having nightmares and awakened crying in the night. Darius always held her, speaking soothingly until she returned to sleep. Using Italian words seemed to comfort her.

Marianne didn't appear to recall what she cried out in the dark, or the things she said, but Darius heard every word as he held her fitful body close to his, crying out for someone she had loved dearly and who was lost to her now. She spoke the name with regret and anguish. The name she cried out in the dark was…Jonathan.

…The squall had sprung up out of nowhere. Jonathan! She ran to the sea as fast as her legs could carry her. The terror pounding inside her chest overrode the bursting need of oxygen for her lungs. Their boat was overturned in the surf. She counted boys. Only two boys! Jonathan? Noooooo…it cannot be true! Where is my Jonathan?

Dear, God, nooooo! I am sorry…sorry…so sorry, Jonath—

"Shhh. Marianne, you're having a bad dream. *Cara*, I am here." Lips kissed her forehead. Strong hands stroked her back.

"Darius?" She awoke quickly, panicked and sweating, trembling in his embrace.

"Yes, darling. It's all right now. You were dreaming…again."

Relaxing into his arms, she became aware of reality. "I am so sorry for disturbing you. I don't know what is wrong with me."

"I think you are sad and missing those whom you have loved and lost."

"…You are probably right, Darius."

"Jonathan? You miss him?" His voice was low and clipped.

"You know about Jonathan?"

"It is his name you cry out in your sleep, Marianne. You loved him."

"Very much. I loved Jonathan the most. He was my light…"

"I understand…you grieve for him," he whispered.

"I do, Darius."

13th August, 1837

Darius knows about Jonathan. I've cried out his name in my sleep. Papa was the last of my destruction of my family. All of them, utterly and completely gone now. I would be too, if not for Darius. I would have nothing to live for. I must tell him…and will have to face up to my great sin, once and for all.

MR

MARIANNE started taking solitary walks along the shore. She tried to do it when Darius was busy for she knew he would not be pleased. He had made her promise she would not walk alone, and she was fully aware of her disobedience as she broke the oath she'd made to her husband.

This day was very much like the day it had happened. The weather typical of late summer, seemingly mild but easily changeable. Marianne had walked out on the rocky headland, purposefully leaving the dogs at home. She needed to be alone today.

This was a favorite spot of hers. Standing on the rocks, she could almost imagine she was on a tiny island, the foamy peaks crashing below. From this vantage point she could scan the ocean horizon and call to him. He was out there somewhere. This was the place she came when she wanted to remember him. His smile. The rakish grin.

The hair and eyes that matched hers.

Marianne was so lost in her musings she didn't take notice of the size of the approaching swell. It exploded into the ledge, blasting a vertical swath of water straight up and onto her. The sheer size of the oversize wave, combined with the rough force, knocked her down, hard. Her feet were blown out from underneath, and she toppled perilously close to the edge.

Her dress, now soaked, weighed heavy and pulled her over. Her feet caught on a ridge of rock, slippery with moss, or she would have gone down. She was inches from going into the churning water below! If she went in, the weight of her garments would sink her. She would drown. Marianne knew the grave danger she was in, but eerily resigned herself if it was to be her fate. *Taken by the sea...just like him...*

And then she thought of Darius and what she needed to say to him. As she dangled there in the cold spray she felt a change. The emotion, the will, the driving need to save herself at all costs. The intense feelings came on her in a rush. She had reasons to live!

Frantically her hands gripped for purchase on the sharp stones above, grasping determinedly until finally gaining a handhold. The jagged rock cut into her skin, but she held on fiercely.

She had to.

Intense resolve strengthened her determination, and

slowly, inch by inch, she pulled herself up onto the flat of the headland.

Lying exhausted from the effort, she counted her blessings and regretted her carelessness.

Thank you, dear God! Thank you…thank you…thank you.

Slowly Marianne rose and shakily took stock of her person. No permanent damage, it seemed. She was very lucky. Hoping she might be able to restore her appearance before Darius should find out what happened, Marianne made her way back to the house as quickly as she could.

She wondered how in the world she'd ever be able to explain the state of her hands, and the bruises that surely bloomed this very moment on her skin.

CHAPTER 14

The Reckoning

"O h, madam! You are hurt and bleeding. We must get you upstairs immediately. Mr. Rourke will want the doctor called. Martha!" Mrs. West was clearly horrified at the sight of her mistress.

"No! I am fine, Mrs. West! Please do not make a fuss. I have merely slipped and scratched my hands. It is mostly water on me. I need a bath and to change my clothes, that is all."

"Your hands need attending to, madam," Mrs. West clucked nervously.

"Could you see to them for me? I really do not see the need to call out the doctor. I don't wish to upset my husband." Marianne pleaded with the housekeeper. "Please, Mrs. West?"

Mrs. West eyed her guardedly. "My dear, if you are injured or at risk to danger, he will be upset regardless."

The housekeeper looked her over some more before softening her harsh frown. "There, there, Mrs. Rourke, let's have Martha get a bath started for you, and I'll tend to those scratches, hmmm?"

The cuts stung painfully under Mrs. West's ministrations, but that was nothing compared to the pain she would feel once Darius knew what she had done.

"Must you tell him, Mrs. West? He'll be so displeased. I hate to burden him with this."

"I think, my dear, you must ask yourself why he would be so displeased," Mrs. West said gently. "He adores you, and you should not take such risks, in your condition." She nodded knowingly. "I am right, am I not?"

"I believe so." Marianne felt a kind of relief at her secret being exposed.

"Then you will have to tell him, madam."

"I know I must. I will tell him myself." She prepared herself for what she knew she must say to him.

"Tell me what?" Darius asked, walking in through the doorway. The color drained out of his face as soon as he got a good look at her, though. "What on earth has happened to you, Marianne?"

"Oh, Darius, I slipped and fell while walking, but it is nothing—just some scratches to my hands. I am fine." She smiled as calmly as she could muster.

He eyed her soaked and filthy dress before fixing them onto her. "Where did you fall as you walked?" His voice was steely and cold.

Marianne winced before answering in a dreaded whisper, "The headland at the shore."

His eyes narrowed, flashing through the slits. His jaw tightened up, but to his credit, he maintained composure. "I'll return when you have been put to rights and are fit to receive me—your husband."

Darius turned from her then and directed his next comment to the housekeeper. "Mrs. West, please inform me at such time my lady wife is restored to her former self so that I might attend her. It appears she has *something* to tell me."

He stalked out of the room without so much as a glance in her direction.

Marianne took in a deep breath, realizing she had been holding it while he was in the room. She could still smell the spice of his cologne after he'd gone.

HER blue shawl draped over a dressing gown, Marianne waited for Darius. As she sat brushing her hair, her hands wouldn't stop trembling and she felt sick to her stomach. Darius was so very angry with her. *The look on his face.* He'd been stricken at the sight of her. She felt chilled to the bone, and her hands ached badly. The reality of what she had done, of what had nearly happened to her, was sobering.

She wanted to please him and be a good wife, but she was failing miserably and had a reckoning coming, she knew. Darius was very good to her, always attentive and considerate, so why then was she compelled to disobey his wishes? That was an easy answer. She didn't deserve all that he gave to her, or the love that he showered upon her. But she wanted to deserve his love. She just didn't know how to begin. Marianne needed to face the truth that she hadn't been honest for a long time, hiding in a world of regret and lost potential.

Darius had changed her, though. Made her feel emotions she couldn't have dreamed she would ever feel again. Made her love…again. Made her love him. She'd fallen in love with her husband, and knew she must tell him everything. It was his right to know about Jonathan, but she was afraid, because of what Darius would think of her once he knew the truth.

Marianne was still sitting in the same spot nearly an hour later when Darius entered her room quietly, walking up behind her as she sat motionless at her dressing table.

The temperature seemed to drop by degrees. He was hard and rigid, like he might want to hit something. She looked up at him through her dressing mirror. They stared at each other for what seemed like an age before he spoke sharply, arms folded. "You have something to tell me, Marianne? Please, I await to hear it."

His icy contempt crushed her. She couldn't hold back the tremors. "You are displeased with me, Darius, I know." She turned in the chair toward him, tentatively reaching out to touch his arm.

His dark eyes blazed down on her so coldly she shrank back and lowered her eyes. He did not like that.

"Oh no, you don't!" He snapped. "You will face me, not shrink away like I'm some monster," he spat, waiting for her to lift her face to him.

God, his eyes were wild, so dark and unbound, but there was something else, too. She saw pain in them. "Darius, you are not a monster, but I see I have made you very angry." She *had* hurt him. And for that she felt even worse. "Listen to what I have to—"

"I am indeed, angry, Marianne. You are aware of my wishes, and yet you defy me. You must not go alone. It is too dangerous. You promised me and then broke your promise. Betrayal…Is that what I get with you? I have to be able to trust you, Marianne. As my wife there must be trust between us." He scrubbed his face in frustration.

"Oh, Darius, I trust you. I would *never* betray you. I just go there to reflect. That is all." She stood and bowed her head, moving ever closer to him.

Letting out an exasperated sigh, he did not offer consolation. "Reflect!" he scoffed. "You risk your safety outrageously. Perched upon the edge of the jetty as you stand above the rough water? Why, a large wave could come and sweep you out to sea in the blink of an eye. From what I can deduce, one nearly did."

"It's what I deserve, really." She mumbled the words very softly, but even so he heard, and he did not like what she'd said.

"What?" he bellowed. "That is a gross mistruth! Marianne!"

Grabbing her by the shoulders, he shook her hard before crushing her to him in a desperate embrace. "Don't ever say such a thing again. I find it obscene. You are more precious to me than anything." She could feel him trembling as he clutched her and then moved her roughly to the bed.

He pushed and down she went onto the mattress, the welcoming softness in sharp contrast with his hard touch. "You are mine," he barked, pointing, his eyes devouring her from the side of the bed where he stood. "Open your gown. Show yourself to me." He looked positively ragged.

"All right, Darius," she said, keeping her eyes on his blistering ones. Slowly, she began to untie her dressing gown, hoping her acquiescence might calm him a little. It didn't. He wasn't inclined to wait and tore it open himself after dropping to the bed with a hiss. The fine French silk fell away at such brutal treatment, exposing all of her to his ravenous gaze.

"These are mine." Cupping her breasts, he dipped his head to cover first one and then the other, swirling over her nipples with his tongue before biting in possession. The bites were a sweet pain that he quickly soothed by following up with soft sucks and tiny licks. "Mine," he murmured between breasts, his lips lingering over her pounding heart.

"Yes," she moaned, arching into his mouth for more of his ragged attentions.

He swept his mouth down, down, down, over ribs and belly and to her cunny. Forceful hands moved quickly to split her thighs, and then he just hovered, motionless, staring at her, almost like he was seeing her sex for the first time. And then she felt his lips come down on her, claiming the burning slit with his tongue. Spearing into her, he teased her clit relentlessly until she felt a possessive but gentle bite there as well. "This is mine, Marianne!"

"Yes!"

Grazing teeth upon the sensitive nub of nerves sent her to dizzying heights. She bucked against the onslaught of his tongue and teeth and lips, a writhing mass of tension and building need. No matter how angry he might be, he was still good to her like this. And she was more than willing to accept the sex, the fucking, the carnality—this she could accept without censure. Accepting his love was harder on her.

She didn't know how he sprung his cock while he was devouring her flesh, but he did somehow. And when he slid into her, hot and hard, the cry she gave was one of pure abandon. Marianne welcomed his driving cock inside her. He completed her, filled her, and satisfied her in a way she now understood, but had been wary of accepting. It didn't take long for his fierce thrusting to push her over the edge and into that abyss of sweet oblivion.

"Yes, Darius...yesssss!"

As he rocked into her feverishly, she sought as much of him as she could possibly get inside her, gripping his hips with her heels, digging in, pressing him closer, further, deeper.

"When my cock is buried in your sweet quim it's where it's meant to be. Mine. Only—for—me!" He fucked into her hard, each stroke a message of dominion over her.

"I know, Darius, I give myself...to you." Marianne welcomed every bit of him in this way. Every stroke, every lick, every suck, every bite, every kiss. And she'd gladly take it all from him.

HER words of surrender caused him to erupt violently,

coming so hard there was pain through his cock when the semen shot up. On and on it surged—his ejaculating. Jets of spunk burst out of him and into her. He marked her body with his very essence. The most primal evidence of claim on a woman, by a man.

"Never risk yourself again. Never again, Marianne," he begged, collapsing in a loose grip against her. Her solemn eyes met his as he held her face close. "I cannot lose you." Whispering in desperation, he closed his eyes. "Please, Marianne, I know I cannot bear it if I were to lose you."

They lay entangled and panting, his body clothed and hers naked, the musky scents of their sex hovering.

"You won't," she said softly.

He realized she was just trying to reassure him though. He stayed quiet, unable to vocalize, vulnerable at the thought of what had nearly happened to her, worried she might do it again, and feeling helpless to prevent it.

"I was careless and distracted. I'll never do it again, go alone to the sea. I am so very sorry. Please forgive me, Darius?"

"Forgive you?" He couldn't believe what he was hearing. "I love...I love you. Can't you understand? I *love* you, Marianne!" Anguish of the heart compressed painfully inside his chest.

She looked up into his eyes, hers full of tears, and touched his face gently. "I know you do, Darius...and I think that you shouldn't—"

He felt excruciatingly hurt at her words, but sacrificed himself anyway. "Oh, *mia cara*, how could I not love you?" Her eyes glimmered at him. "You are everything I could ever want, or ever need to make my life complete." He whispered the rest. "Marianne, I think, have always thought, and will always know, that you are someone very perfect."

Burying her face into his chest, she rocked back and forth. "Darius, I am not—"

"I know you cannot love me back. I know, Marianne. I am well aware of what I have done to you."

An expression of confusion crossed her features. "I was going to say, 'I am not *perfect*.' You think me perfect when I am not, Darius! Why do you always say such to me? And what is it that you believe you have done to me anyway?" She shook her head at him in question.

"I have done you wrong, Marianne. I wanted you, for so long. In my bed. To possess you. To have you. I wanted your body and your soul, so it has been for a very long time. You granted my greatest wishes when you married me and put all of that within my grasp. You gave all of yourself so freely. But I found I wanted more. More than I know you can give to me."

"What do you want, Darius?"

"Something you do not have for me, but for another you have lost."

"Love? You really want my love? Why do you not tell me to say it to you? I have waited for you to tell me to say the words, but you do not."

She paused, just looking and waiting for him, her blue eyes blazing.

It made him wary. He wasn't going to direct her on this. No. He would not. There would be no more telling her what to say, either. It hurt to do that now. He'd gambled with her and lost.

"Can you not tell me to say, 'I love you?'" she asked. "I will give you that. I want to."

"Not this time, dear one. Not this time."

Tears spilled down her face. "Darius?"

"No!" he shouted. "I will not do that to you!"

"Do what? What have you done to me? I don't understand you!" she wailed.

"Shhh." He stroked her face, getting close up to her. "Oh, *cara,* it is all my fault. I coerced you—gave you no real choice in marrying me. I owned all the debt from your father for months. I planned for his eventual ruin. I called it in when you turned me down the first time. Knowing that you would be mine and I would have you finally, I did not care about the deception. Before I even knew what I was about, you had ensnared my heart in totality. I found myself in love with a woman who waited for me to tell her what to do, to say, to feel, and it quickly grew to be most unsatisfying...for my heart. I could tell you to say that you loved me, but I learned you cannot dominate a heart, Marianne. Those three words must be given freely to have meaning." He felt his bottom lip begin to tremble. "I am sorry for what I have done, but never sorry for loving you. Marianne, in my heart, you are master, and I am servant." He kissed her on the forehead with one gentle kiss.

She was quiet a long time before she spoke, the silence engulfing them like a cloak. "I have to tell you something, Darius. The reason I am unworthy…the reason I am…as I am."

"Unworthy?" How could she believe herself unworthy? "No, Marianne, please don't say that—"

"—Darius, do you know why? Why I wanted your direction?"

"No, *cara,* I don't. I just sensed it from you. And being so attracted, I was determined to have you for myself. I had to be the one to give you what you needed, and I was so desperate to win you, I would have done anything. Your father's decline made it very easy for me, too easy, I know."

He knew what he must ask. And he was afraid of her answer. And his heart hurt terribly. Still, he had to know. "Marianne, are you the way you are because of…Jonathan?"

Marianne gasped when the name crossed his lips. "Yes…it *is* because of him. He is the reason." She got quiet again, the silence hanging, waiting for words.

Finally, she started to tell her story. "Jonathan...I failed him. I am responsible. I as good as killed him. His death is on me, and I confess it is a struggle. 'Tis why I walk on the headland sometimes, to remember him and beg his forgiveness. For my mistake."

"Mistake?"

"Oh yes, the worst kind of error. My brother died because of me. Because of a decision I made. I was at fault, and he died for it. My whole family followed him...really."

"Brother? Jonathan was your brother?" Darius thought his heart might leap out of his chest. *Brother...He was her brother...*

She nodded in reflection. "My baby brother. He was so beautiful." She looked weary and very sad.

"I had no idea," he breathed. "Darling, you are tired and have been through a frightening ordeal." He kissed her ravaged hands reverently. "Your poor hands. Thank God they were able to pull you up. Precious, precious hands." Drawing her into his arms, he found her shawl and covered her up with it. He savored the warmth of her body and the knowledge that she was safe with him now, that he had not lost her today.

Thank you, dear God.

"Marianne, will you tell me about Jonathan? I would like to know, if you can bear to speak of him."

CHAPTER 15

The Unburdening

Darius held on to Marianne, secure in his arms, and never wanted to let go. He listened to her story…

"My father was doting and amusing when I was young. He teased me, saying I could not possibly be his little girl for being so solemn. I wanted a brother or sister so badly. When I was six years old, my wish came true, and Jonathan was born. I adored that child so much. He was beautiful, the light of our lives, but very willful." Her voice broke. "When…he was ten, Jonathan left us, and it changed everything."

She gave in to tears then, pressing up against his chest for comfort. Darius was grateful that she seemed to need him and gladly held her securely next to his thudding heart. After a time, he asked gently, "Can you tell me, darling? I do not know the story of your brother. I want to understand." He waited for her to continue, patiently caressing her back.

"Jonathan went out in the rowboat with some other boys when he was expressly told 'no' by Papa. I surprised him behind the house when I caught him sneaking off. He pressed his fingers to his lips, begging me to keep his secret." She shook her head. "I couldn't deny him anything, so I didn't expose him to Papa. They went out in the rowboat and a squall came up from nowhere. The waves capsized their boat and Jonathan was swept away—his body never found. The sea claimed him."

"Oh, darling, I am so sorry." Like clouds parting for the illuminating sun, Darius was finally beginning to understand his wife.

"You see, it is my fault. I should have told Papa he was leaving in the boat. Papa would have stopped him, and Jonathan would be alive still. It was an appalling mistake, and I made it. The loss of Jonathan crushed Mamma. She died but a year later, and Papa began to take to drink. I tried to care for him the best I could, but I was unable to save Papa in the end anyway. Everyone I love leaves me eventually."

"Oh, *cara*, I had no idea about any of this. It happened after I left Somerset." He kissed her on the forehead, caressing the back of her head, weaving through her hair.

"Marianne, you were but a child yourself. It was a tragic accident. Surely you see that you cannot bear the burden of guilt upon your shoulders alone?"

"I was old enough to know better, and I was afraid to tell my parents that I'd seen him and let him go. No one ever knew that part of it. If they had, they would have hated me for it. I was afraid to tell them and lose their love…and be all alone…" She broke down and sobbed in great heaves against his chest, and it was some time before she could continue. He kept stroking her softly; ever patient, knowing she'd keep going when she was able.

"'Tis why I feel unworthy of you and everything you've given me. 'Tis why I craved for you to tell me what to do, to think, and to feel. If you tell me, I am not responsible for decisions. I am safe. I can just float in the sensation without worry I'll make the wrong choice. If something bad happens it won't be my fault. Do you understand, Darius? That's why I needed you to tell me. It gave me some solace from the burden of guilt…"

She stopped speaking, and he just held her some more, hoping like hell she could feel how much he did love her. So many things were now clear about her. The mysterious detachment, her willing submission to him, her giving nature, the difficulty in accepting demonstrations of affection and gifts from him all made sense to him now. In all things, she was trying to atone for something that couldn't be atoned.

He spoke in a dead calm, hoping to impart reason into her opinions of herself. "I understand, Marianne, but I also know you need to let that guilt go. The burden of it is killing you slowly. It cannot help Jonathan or you. Jonathan is long at peace, and you have a life to live." He clutched her a little tighter. "I need you, and you are most worthy, in my eyes. It changes nothing. I love you still and could never let you go anyway. You'll have to put up with me until I go to my grave."

It was quiet for a minute or more. Who knew? He'd bared it all. His soul was laid out raw and exposed. She had demons to conquer, and only she could banish them, really. He could love and support her, but he couldn't bring her brother back for her, or force her to let go of the guilt. The silence stretched on, and with each passing second his heart sank into deeper distress.

She pulled back from his chest and reached for his face, cradling it in both of her soft hands. He felt a flicker of hope when her beautiful lips began to speak.

"And then you came along, Darius, and loved me. Strangely, I know I have hope that I might be free now, and it's only because of you. The accident today helped to show me how much I have to live for. I didn't want to die. I couldn't. So I fought to pull myself to safety with every ounce of strength I could muster. I had to live, you see, because I have two very important reasons…"

149

His breath caught. "Yes?"

She nodded, her blue eyes glowing beautifully. Taking his hand, she pressed it to the soft, flat plane of her stomach. "I must live so I can be mother to our child. A child I want very much. A child I will love, fiercely."

"Dear God! You are certain?"

"Yes, Darius. You will be a father." The look of joy on her face was worth more to him than anything save for the precious gift she was giving him by her declaration.

He bent down to whisper and kiss over her belly. "Our baby is here, growing inside you right now. Oh, you will be such a loving mother. Our sweet child is blessed, you know."

He froze when he thought about how hard he'd just taken her and panicked. "Damnation! I was too rough with you. I am sorry, *cara*!" He looked up from her belly, nearly incapacitated with fear. "Did I hurt—"

"—DARIUS, I am perfectly well. You did not hurt me, and I like your loving me just the way you do it." She pulled him back up from her stomach to her lips and kissed him softly. "It is very early yet, and we won't have to worry about changing our habits for some time."

"Just the same, I intend to take very good care of you and be ever so careful." He smiled at her, but she could detect a slight regret in the expression.

Marianne thought she knew why. "Darius, aren't you going to ask me?"

His eyes shuttered. "Ask you what, *cara*?"

"My other reason. I said I had two important reasons to live. Our baby is one reason."

He whispered without meeting her eyes. "What is the other reason, Marianne?" His voice carried the identifiable fear to hear whatever it was, but compelled to know anyway.

His eyes stayed down as she began to speak. "Darius, I love that you make me feel cherished. I love that you want me and say I am precious to you. I love that you need my body fiercely. I love the closeness with you. I love that you want me to be the mother of your children. You've given all of that to me, even when I thought I shouldn't deserve any of it. And even though it still may be hard for me sometimes…to let go of the guilt, I want to try to put the past away. I want to hold on to you and your love, for our sake and our child's." She brought their hands to her belly together. "You are the best of men, Darius Rourke, and there is something else you need to know…"

She altered her voice, demand evident in her tone. "Look at me, Darius. You want to look at me."

He lifted his dark eyes, silver flecks glittering, and focused on her.

"I am going to tell you what you want to say. You want to say it, Darius. You do." She nodded determinedly. "Say, 'Marianne loves Darius with all of her heart.' You want to say it, because it is the truth. Tell me, Darius. Say those words."

He trembled a little, his bottom lip moving, distinct against the sharp lines of his jaw. This beautiful man, her man, her wonderful, loving husband, trembled before her, and the knowledge just split her heart apart…with even more love for him.

"Say it to me," she commanded.

"Marianne loves…Darius with all of her heart." He pushed the sentence out on a breath, his eyes growing shiny.

"She does indeed." Marianne smiled at her husband with all of the love she had to give to him, and felt it shimmering out from her like a radiant aura. "So very much, for he is easy to love."

"Will she tell me often?"

Marianne slowly nodded.

"I don't think I can ever tire from hearing you tell me. In fact, it is what I need," Darius said. "I need to hear it from you as often as you need to hear it from me. I s'pose we should be awash in declarations of love."

"Fair is fair."

His eyes glowed at her. "Start now."

She leaned up for a kiss, whispering at his lips, "*Ti amo,*

Darius. I—love—you."

He cradled her face and kept her close. "You *are* perfect, you know? My Marianne. My love most beloved...*il mia amore più cara.*"

24th September, 1837

The most beautiful gift was given to me today. Darius is so wonderful all the time with his thoughtfulness. He had the stonemason make a statue, of a mermaid angel, carved specifically for the garden wall. Jonathan's tribute there for me to look at, and think of him fondly in his way, wherever he may now be. He is free...and in some small part, I feel very much the same.

MR

EPILOGUE

The Blessing

14th April, 1838

Darius awoke with a start. Marianne wasn't next to him in the bed. God, would the panic of finding her missing ever abate? He doubted it. Propping himself up on his elbows, he scanned the room in the dim light of daybreak. There she was. Wrapped in her blue shawl, sitting on the chaise before the fire. She sat very still. So still he would think her asleep if her back wasn't so ramrod straight.

He kept his eyes on her as he got out of bed and donned his robe. He could see her shoulders moving, just barely, and in a predictable rhythm that followed steady breaths. He came to her slowly and knelt on the rug at her feet. She kept her eyes closed, but he could tell she was wide awake. Her hands rested one on each thigh. He lowered his head onto her lap at her knees and felt the gentle weight of her hand touch him, beginning a soft, rhythmic pattern of trailing through his hair with her fingers.

Words weren't necessary. Communication flowed through to their minds from their hearts, or so it seemed to him. Darius put his energy into savoring this precious moment with her because he suspected the time was very near. Everything was equipped, and had been for weeks. They'd pored over books together and prepared themselves with as much knowledge as they could glean. All that remained was the experience and for nature to take its proper course as had been done by women for millennia. He cared only about one woman though. His. He would not press her now. She would tell him when she was ready.

The finger-combing went on for a good five minutes, when she froze abruptly. He could feel her legs tighten under his cheek and her back stiffen against the seat of the chaise. Her fingers gripped a hank of his hair and formed a fist. She stayed like that until the spasm ceased, and he felt her relax.

Darius lifted his head and looked up at Marianne. Her eyes were still closed. He waited, watching her even breaths raise and lower the big swell of her belly. Their child safe inside her body. Her eyes snapped open and captured his. A very intense indigo-blue gaze held him—the gaze of a female warrior.

"Darius?"

"Yes, *mia cara*?"

"It's time. Tell Mrs. West we need the doctor and the midwife. Our child will be born this day…"

The next fourteen hours were not a stroll through the garden for Darius. But he wouldn't allow for acknowledgement of his own struggles because the strength that Marianne displayed while fighting to bring their baby into the world just stripped him down, bare to the bone, humbled at her feet. He had pause to consider how she had looked at him early this morning when she'd said it was time. He'd thought her a warrior queen then. The metaphor was an apt one because she was in battle now sure as any soldier could ever be.

Watching Marianne bear down through another pain, he felt drops of sweat roll down his back and his hand squeezed in a bone-crushing grip that defied possibility. Her strength was amazing! Hell, all women were amazing in their ability to create new life. The notion they were considered "the weaker sex" was sheer idiocy in his view. Maybe men who held such beliefs should present themselves at a birth and see if their opinions might not merit drastic revision.

He exhaled in relief when the birth-pain eased and she flopped back against him and the pillows that propped her. Marianne was set up in her bed, and he at her side, bracing her through every gripping contraction, and despite doctors' and midwives' disinclination to allow a father into a birthing room, he was going nowhere. Marianne wanted him, and he'd promised, so he was here for the duration. She so rarely asked for anything, that when she did so, he was more determined than ever to give her what she wanted. "So brave, *mia cara.*" He blotted the sweat and tears away and whispered at her ear. "That's another done." He pressed his lips to her damp brow. "You're so strong. Breathe deep now, before the next one comes." He looked helplessly at Dr. Winslow, who arched a brow at him as if to say, *"I'd really like it if you took your irritating arse out of here."* Darius just shook his head in a definitive "no."

"Thirsty…" Marianne panted, breaking through the tension and meeting his eyes, bringing him back to her.

"Of course, *cara.*" He held a glass of water to her lips, trying to hurry before the next pain took hold. In less than two swallows she was seized by another contraction—the biggest one so far. She bit out an agonized cry that rent his heart to further shreds.

Dr. Winslow perked up, but retained his steady calm. "Ah. There it is. The head, I can see the head now. Mrs. Rourke, time to push. Now, my dear. Hard as you can.

Your baby wants to meet you," he sang. "Mr. Rourke, sit her up please…"

What followed next was the hardest thing he'd ever had to witness, but would not have missed for anything in the world. Holding her upright and steady, he endured every cry and forceful push and streaming tear, hating that she must suffer so, and wishing he could bear it for her.

But their reward came in due time. Those last few moments of Marianne's intense pain evaporated into greatest joy when Dr. Winslow proclaimed, "Congratulations! You have a son."

MARIANNE had never been more beautiful, nor had he ever seen her more radiant, or perceived more joy in her than right now at this moment, holding their son in her loving arms. Darius hung back at the doorway and watched, loathe to break the enchantment of the moment. He felt like an intruder.

Earlier, he'd found it prudent to excuse himself while the midwife, Mrs. West, and Martha, got down to the business of post-birth necessities such as bathing the baby and seeing to Marianne. Some intimacies were best left to the women, after all. Refreshed in clean bedding and wearing a new gown, Marianne had her shawl over her shoulders. Dark coffee waves spilled over the sea-blue silk, the way he'd always loved her hair best, tied with a ribbon to the side. Her twilight eyes could look no further than the infant in her arms though. She simply gazed, looking totally in love and in awe of what she held. Her thumb brushed back and forth in a soft caress on the creamy blanket that swaddled him.

"Aren't you going to come in? We've been waiting for you." Her voice was low, but welcoming, as if she could sense his hesitation, and she never took her eyes off the baby. "Your son wishes to meet his papa."

God, how he loved her! How she perceived that he needed some reassurance and gave it so generously. He came to the edge of the bed and saw his son. *He had a son!* A tiny pink face topped with dark, fine curls peeked from the blanket, a miniature hand and five fingers clasping the fabric's edge. Bow-shaped baby lips made phantom sucks as their son dreamt in his mother's arms. Such emotion flowed into him; he'd never have believed it possible to *feel* so deeply. They had made this tiny person and would always be bound to him by blood. Darius would lay down his life to protect these two people, and the knowledge of that fact made his heart swell in his chest.

"He is beautiful. Just like his mother."

"Just like his father." She cooed at the baby. "He looks like you, Darius."

"You think so?" He tilted his head, smiling down at

his son, pride filling him.

"I know so. I've been memorizing his features. His chin, that strong brow are a mirror of yours. Not quite sure about his nose yet—" She stopped suddenly and looked up. "How about you come into the bed with us and get a closer look."

He eased down next to them and was grateful for the soft cushion, for his body suddenly registered the effects of this arduous day.

"Now, you've got to support his neck for him and just tuck him against your chest," she announced, transferring the precious bundle.

"What are you—I—I—am to hold him?" he sputtered. "He—he—is so small and fragile—" He found his words resisting the idea, but his body had a different response as his hands just reached out and brought the baby close.

"Yes, Darius, you are to hold him, and he's not that fragile."

"Oh." Pure, innocent, perfect love was what he felt for this small, new person in his arms. He fell in total love with him all in an instant. Darius brushed his finger against the tiny hand, which responded by gripping around it with force. "My God," he gasped. "You're right. He's not fragile, I feel his strength. He is so strong! Our son is very strong. Such a strong little man you are," he crooned, "aren't you, my son?"

Marianne laughed at him. Just a small, satisfied laugh, but he didn't care. He had a son…and they were holding on to one another! Life was good.

"You know, Darius, we're going to have to come up with a name for this little prince."

"I can think of only one name that would suit, *cara*."

"And?"

"Don't you know?" He met her eyes. "I think you know the name, Marianne." He smiled at the woman he loved. "Only if you wish it, but understand that I think the name will honor him and honor our son, both at the same time."

She leaned into him, resting her head on his chest, reached out and gently touched the silky fine hair of their son's head. "Then, Jonathan, you are. Jonathan Darius Rourke. Our Jonathan." They enjoyed the quiet together, content to watch Jonathan sleep, his pure baby scent an ambrosia of fragrance, hovering over them. Her beautiful voice floated softly to him. "I love you, Darius. And I love our Jonathan. Thank you. For both of you."

"As I love the both of you, *cara*." He kissed the top of her head. "How are you? Are you well? You were so amazingly brave and strong and magnific—"

"—I am perfect."

Now it was his turn to laugh. "You've never said as much to me before."

"But it's true. You asked me how I am. I *am* perfect.

Perfect child. Perfect husband. Perfect love." She smiled that half-mast smile of hers.

"Do you mean it? Truly?" Darius asked.

"Oh yes, with every beat of my heart," Marianne answered.

DARIUS became a believer in heavenly blessings after that day. As the years unfolded, he lived his life in good measure, but thinking of his wife in the very same way he always had, for in his heart she had never changed. Marianne was still as he had found her to be from the very first. Still beautiful and mysterious, still loving and generous, still taking his breath away with her unending gifts so freely given to him.

She was all of that for him and more. Marianne was his reason for being. He had found his true perfect passion. Darius Rourke knew he was a blessed man.

28th May, 1838

I have written of the weight of my guilt many times upon these pages. Moments when I was consumed so greatly, I could not see a future of any kind ever becoming a possibility. A heavy burden, carried for years until one person helped me to cast it away. I know there will be times I feel guilt still cloaking me, but for the first time, I have some clarity of forethought to understand how my burdens did nothing to help any of those who have been lost to me.

Darius saved me from myself. Of this, I am very aware. Without his love, I am certain I would not breathe to this day, nor would my heart beat within my breast.

There is great beauty in the simplicity of giving oneself to another in trust, and allowing them to hold you up. My Darius taught me this lesson. From the beginning, he could really see me. I believe he is the only person to ever see inside my soul. A rare gift, which has served to give back to me—my life.

He gave me our precious Jonathan, and also the gift of serenity in letting my J. go. I now know J. is at a peaceful place, where what transpires in this earthly realm, is but a speck floating along in the oceans of time. In the hours of the darkest kind, Darius has ever been my light. My lover who saw inside my battered soul and freed me.

M R

THE END

If you enjoyed this book, please consider leaving a review. Thank you for reading!

If you'd like to join us, there is a discussion group on Facebook for the book. The link is below.

DISCUSS The Passion of Darius
https://www.facebook.com/groups/DiscussPassionofDarius/

If you enjoy Contemporary Romance, read about the occupants of Stonewell Court 175 years later in my **BLACKSTONE AFFAIR** *series.*

BOOKS BY RAINE MILLER

The Blackstone Affair

NAKED, BOOK 1
ALL IN, BOOK 2
EYES WIDE OPEN, BOOK 3
CHERRY GIRL, BOOK 3.5
RARE and PRECIOUS THINGS, BOOK 4

Historical Prequels to The Blackstone Affair

The PASSION of DARIUS
The UNDOING of a LIBERTINE

ABOUT THE AUTHOR

Raine has been reading romance novels since she picked up that first Barbara Cartland paperback at the tender age of thirteen. She thinks it was *The Flame is Love* from 1975. And it's a safe bet she'll never stop reading romance novels because now she writes them too. Granted, Raine's stories are edgy enough to turn Ms. Cartland in her grave, but to her way of thinking, a tall, dark and handsome hero never goes out of fashion. Never! A former teacher turned full- time writer of sexy romance stories, is how she fills her days. Raine has a prince of a husband, and two brilliant sons to pull her back into the real world if the writing takes her too far away. Her sons know she likes  to write stories, but have never asked to read any. (Raine is so very grateful about this.) She loves to hear from readers and chat about the characters in her books. You can connect with Raine on Facebook or visit her at **www.RaineMiller.com** to sign up for updates and see what she's working on now.

Notes

CPSIA information can be obtained at www.ICGtesting.com
Printed in the USA
LVOW06s2028240215

428171LV00004B/63/P